W9-DBN-172

FOLLOW THE TOFF

JOHN CREASEY

FOLLOW
THE TOFF

Walker and Company
New York

CONTENTS

v

vi

CONTENTS

PROLOGUE

ALL his life, the Honourable Richard Rollison had been eager to help the young and the beautiful, as well as the old and the deserving, and when he was asked for help by Alice Day, he did not hesitate to give it.

Alice Day was really in trouble, for she and her new husband had been swindled out of nearly two hundred pounds.

"And it's all we had, Mr. Rollison," Alice said. "It's every penny. Mike had paid for our passage money to Australia, and this two hundred was all we had to live on until he got a job out there. It's a tragedy."

In its way it was.

"Now tell me again just how it happened," said Rollison.

"Even now it hardly seems possible," said Alice. "We'd been to Paris for the week-end to see Mike's sister. We went partly to say goodbye, and, partly to get this money from Gillian. It was the repayment of an old debt. Of course, Gillian gave it to Mike in French money and we planned to change it when we got back to England. Then a man at the station in Paris said he could give us a shilling in the pound extra, and—well, we fell for it. The cash he had looked all right. No one at the customs asked how much we'd got, and it wasn't until we got home and tried to spend some that we discovered it was all forged."

"I see," said Rollison. "When are you due to sail, do you say?"

"Tomorrow," said Alice. "Oh, I know it's impossible

to do anything in the time. Lady Gloria said that if any-one could, you would."

"And I will," declared Rollison firmly. "I'll buy the forged money, and find the man who cheated you. He'll cough up."

Alice's eyes grew radiant; but suddenly they dimmed. "But how can you find him? How on earth—"

"You describe him and I'll do it," Rollison said. "Height, appearance, what he was dressed in—"

"I can try," said Alice, dubiously. "I was so excited that I hardly noticed. Mike is probably better at that than I. Mr Rollison, you aren't making an excuse to give us this money, are you?"

"No," said Rollison and he wasn't; his Aunt Gloria was, but there was no need to say so. "I'll get it back all right, I've had a very slack time lately, I could do with some mental exercise, and it's a long time since I spent a few days in Paris. Now, let's hurry. I'll draw a cheque, and if you get a move on you'll reach the bank in time to change it for cash."

That was how the case began.

And Alice's Mike gave a clearer description of the man who had swindled them than Alice had expected; it was a very good description indeed.

1

FOLLOW THE TOFF

It was not the first time that the Honourable Richard Rollison had been followed. It would not be the last. It had happened in many cities, and more than once before in this fair city of Paris in the Spring. It had happened by by day and by night, on land, on sea and in the air. Rollison himself, if challenged, would have said that he believed that every possible variation of the theme had been developed, yet on this day in May he knew that he had been wrong.

It was the first time that such beauty had followed him.

The beauty was undoubtedly English, although he had not yet heard her speak. She had that curiously indefinable quality, perhaps more rightly air, about her. It was not only the supreme simplicity of her black and white check suit, the coat short-waisted, the skirt just long enough to be in fashion, and to show most of the shapeliness of her legs. Nor was it those long, slim legs, or her height—five feet eight or nine he judged—or her complexion, although undoubtedly her complexion had something to do with it.

It was a little bit of everything.

She had followed him from the Café de Paris, of which it was said that if one sat long enough one would meet all the rest of the world; in fact at the Café de Paris he had first realised that she had been interested in him. She had walked past the long lines of wicker tables and chairs, most

9

of them empty. The glass screens of winter had been whisked away and the spring sunshine not only made life serene but almost made it possible to forget the surging traffic, the growl and snarl of engines, the bark and clatter of taxis, the all-pervading stench of petrol fumes mingling with even worse from diesel oil. As Rollison had sat over late *petit déjeuner*, wondering why the French who made the world's worst coffee had a reputation for making it so well, and why the English, who made the world's best, were supposed to make the worst, the woman had walked past. She had looked at him and then walked quickly away. He had not been in a hurry, however; such grace and slenderness and beauty were all too rare. He watched her go, a little pensive because he doubted whether he would ever have an excuse to meet her, perhaps not even to see her again. But soon she had turned back from the corner by the Place de l'Opéra. That in itself had not been unusual; people often walked as far as that, and then turned back. This time Rollison pretended to take no notice of her, but observed that she stared intently at him, and looked back at him several times.

By then, Rollison's interest had become much stronger. For one thing, he realised just how remarkable the woman was to look at, and remarkable women could usually make his heart beat a little faster. For another thing, he was beginning to feel sure that she had recognised him and wanted to talk but could not summon up the courage—if courage was the word.

He could make it easy for her, or make it comparatively hard. He would have made it easy but for the little man.

This little man was almost certainly the man who had swindled Alice Day, who was now on her way to Australia. He fitted Mike's description to a T, and he spent some time at stations, outside night-clubs and other tourist

haunts, offering money at a good rate of exchange. Only
a few people seemed to deal with him, and Rollison
planned to catch him red-handed with forged notes. Now
this same man was following the Englishwoman, and
Rollison did not try to guess whether she knew it or not. If
she knew, she was taking no notice—unless, of course,
awareness of the surveillance of the little man kept her
from approaching Rollison boldly.

It was a mildly intriguing situation, and quite enter-
taining; it would have been amusing but for the woman's
obvious anxiety. Beauty in distress was never even remotely comic. An ordinary man, assessing the situation
as Rollison assessed it, would almost certainly have found
an excuse to talk to the woman, and might possibly have
tried to shoo the little man off. There were times when
Rollison—known as the Toff to the police of seven conti-
nents and to the criminals of six, would have taken such
direct action, but this was not one of them. He had two
reasons for being intrigued: his Aunt Gloria's two hundred
pounds, and this beauty.

At ten minutes to eleven the woman was some way
along the Boulevard des Capucines in the direction of the
Madeleine, and the little man was fifty yards behind
her. Every motor car in Paris seemed to be crammed
into the road which had seemed wide in the days of horse
carriages.

Rollison called for his bill, paid, and allowed himself
to be swept across the road with a surge of human beings
all racing to make sure that they reached the opposite
pavement before the roaring monsters of iron and steel
were unleashed at the whirl of a gendarme's white baton
or a trill on his hidden whistle. Once on the far side,
Rollison watched the woman, and he was tall enough to
see and be seen without difficulty. When he was sure that

she had spotted him, he discontinued a tentative interest in a window which exhibited every refinement of feminine foundation in black, pink, and pale mauve silk, and strolled towards the Madeleine. The woman walked in the same direction on the other side of the road. She followed him along the street opposite the church of the mammoth pillars towards the arid wastes of the Place de la Concorde, and then by devious dangerous routes towards the Seine. Now and again Rollison made sure that not only the woman but the little man was behind him. Then, as if at a loose end, he crossed to the Rue de Rivoli and became one of the thousands of tourists promenading beneath the arches and seduced by a million model Eiffel Towers and a thousand Joan of Arcs. The woman drew closer. Rollison dawdled. He thought that this time she would speak, for she actually passed within a yard of him. He imagined that he could hear her breathing agitatedly—but she passed without stopping.

Rollison continued to study a window resplendent in Arab leatherwork and Moroccan silver, as the little man drew nearer.

This little man was quite remarkable too. The task of following an individual through a city the size of Paris is not easy even for those people physically adapted to it, but he was only about five feet two inches high. Heads and shoulders of all sizes, chests and bosoms of all shapes, arms and even hands got in his way, but doggedly he kept on the trail. He wasn't remarkable in any other way; in fact he was the type who could easily get lost in a crowd. Rollison judged him to be French, not only because he was blue-jowled and wore a slightly faded beret, but because he chain-smoked Skol cigarettes; only a Frenchman could have such hardihood and courage. He had a pinched nose which looked as if it had been pushed to one side, and a little bloodless mouth, a surprisingly square and thrusting chin, and a well cut brown suit; the beret did not quite match up to this. He wore suede shoes too of dark brown, a shade darker than the brown of his suit. All of this Mike had described very well.

The woman had gone by. The little Frenchman was following. Rollison judged his moment, and stepped into the little man's path. There was a ridiculous contretemps of dither and dart, as if each man was trying to give way to the other, but in fact Rollison did not mean to give way until the moment was right. So they collided. A woman gasped: "Oo!" as only someone born in Blackpool could. The little man reeled back, as if dazed. Rollison gave a dazzling smile and apologised, and allowed the man to pass. Then, watched by at least a dozen people, he darted his left hand towards the inside of his coat pocket. Every Method school of acting would have approved his performance. He looked startled, aghast, appalled, angry, and finally vengeful. Then in the clearest and loudest of English he called:

"*Stop thief!*"

Fifty people looked round, mostly English and American all open-mouthed, some ready to fling themselves foward with great courage, most trying to make sure that they could get out of the way. "*Stop thief!*" cried Rollison again, and moved with astonishing rapidity through the crowd towards the little Frenchman, who had not hurried and had not looked round. The Englishwoman was now staring at those massed gilt models of the Eiffel Tower, the Notre Dame, and Joan of Arc on a gilded statue, the original of which was only a hundred yards away.

Rollison pounced on him, gripped his shoulder, and spun him round. The man gaped. A gendarme standing in the roadway trilled on his whistle, swung his baton

and charged forward. A crowd collected, most of them
people at a safe distance, but one sturdy Yorkshireman and
his wife came to Rollison's support.

"Is that reet?" the Yorkshireman demanded. "Did he
take summat out of thy pocket?"

"The scoundrel stole my wallet," asserted Rollison, and
as he spoke the gendarme came up and rested a hand on
the butt of his revolver, warningly, and machine-gunned
a dozen questions.

"I don't understand a word you're saying," lied Rollison hotly. "This man pretended to collide with me just
now, and stole my wallet."

"That is not so," declared the little man, in highly
accented English. "Eet is the big lie."

The gendarme demanded, in French, to know what
exactly had happened. Rollison tapped his pocket, thrust
his hand inside, drew it out empty, and declared:

"*He—stole—my—wallet.*"

"*That—ees—the—lie.*"

"*M'sieu, je demande que vous parlez Francais.*"

"He stole—"

The little man turned to the gendarme and poured out
an earnest, even an impassioned denial—he had not
touched Rollison's wallet, he had not touched Rollison.
He was a law-abiding citizen, he was not to be insulted,
he—

"*He stole my wallet!*" roared Rollison.

"Eeeh, lad, better leave it to me," said the Yorkshireman, and began to talk in surprisingly colloquial French
in spite of an unbelievable admixture of Yorkshire accent.
Even the little man was silenced, and the gendarme
appeared to begin to understand. As the Yorkshireman
finished, the gendarme held his baton at the ready and
spoke with the air of a Solomon:

"If this man stole your wallet, he will have it with him now."

Rollison just saved himself from agreeing in French and asked the Yorkshireman:

"What's all the blathering about?"

"He says that if this man stole tha wallet he'd still have it on him."

"Fair enough," agreed Rollison. "So why not search him?"

"You look, you see—*nothing*," declared the little Frenchman. He gripped the edges of his coat, and flung it open at arms' length, as if he hoped to be able to take off and fly with these homemade wings. He was undoubtedly convinced that the wallet was not there, perhaps because he had never met Rollison before. The gendarme stared, the Yorkshireman gaped and glanced with earthy satisfaction at Rollison. A dozen other people craned forward to see Rollison's crocodile leather wallet showing fully an inch above the Frenchman's pocket.

"Eeeh, lad," said the Yorkshireman, "tha'd best leave talking to me. Just tell me where thou 'rt staying and I'll talk to copper for thee."

"I don't know what I would have done without you," said Rollison warmly. "I'm staying at the *George V*, and . . ."

The little Frenchman was staring at Rollison as if damning him to everlasting hell, but there was a shocked expression in his brown eyes, and his expression seemed to suggest that he could not really believe any of this. The wallet was now in the possession of the gendarme, who was counting out notes with increasing wonderment and respect, for Rollison had changed a substantial traveller's cheque that morning. The whole performance took another twenty minutes, before the wallet was back with

Rollison, together with the money, and the gendarme,
reinforced by two others, led the hapless little man off.
The Yorkshireman had contrived to save Rollison the
chore of going with them to make a charge; he would be
called upon by an *agent de police* at three o'clock that afternoon, and would be required later that same afternoon or
tomorrow morning to visit a magistrate at the Courts of
Justice.

"I really don't know how to thank you," Rollison said
to the Yorkshireman, earnestly.

"I can tell 'ee how," the man said. He was short and
stumpy, had sandy coloured hair, a florid face and the
brightest of bright blue eyes. "Tha can tell me what it's
all about, Mr. Rollison, when tha've time for it. It isn't
every day a man has a chance to help the Toff in person.
I'm at the Grand Hotel, Room 791, and I'd be reet glad if
tha'd give me a call some time today or tomorrow."

Rollison gaped at him.

The Yorkshireman winked, took his wife's plump hand,
and said: "Come on, Elsie, we'll never get shopping done
if we stay gowping here all day," and led his wife away.
Rollison watched two broad and fleshy backs, two thick
red necks, two pairs of skin-tight trousers, the woman's of
a red and green check unbelievably tighty across an
enormous beam. He was so astonished at being recognised
that for a moment he forgot the Englishwoman who had
started all this hocus pocus. Until that moment he had
wondered where she was and what he could do to find
her.

He need not have worried.

She was pretending to look into a window filled with
countless dainty and impracticable shoes for midget feet,
but twice glanced round at Rollison, who strolled on,
followed by at least a dozen sightseers. He was followed

by the Englishwoman as soon as he was ten yards past her.

He wondered whether she would be bold enough to approach him now that the little Frenchman was out of the way.

2

REQUEST

THE Tuileries Gardens were cool and restful to the eye, even the small children who kicked up miniature clouds of dust from the paths and ran wild among the flower beds were not wholly unpleasing. On either side of the great courtyard of the Louvre, women sat on wooden benches, knitting as they chattered, some jogging a baby carriage up and down to the rhythm of quick moving fingers, some singing lullabies, some restraining toddlers by tinkling reins fastened to the captive benches. Forming an inner ring, a mass of parked cars provided the only sight hard upon the eyes. The sun shone upon the shiny tops and heat haze shimmered towards the blue sky.

Rollison strolled towards the main entrance to the Louvre, and the Englishwoman was now coming through one of the arches. It looked for a moment as if she were going to be mown down by a growling green bus, but it swung aside like a tank and she was oblivious of it. No one appeared to have replaced the small man, who was undoubtedly protesting his innocence before a sceptical Inspecteur at the local Commisariat de Police.

Rollison stepped inside the entrance, bought his ticket, went towards the stairs and was almost carried down by a torrent of small children obeying a skeleton thin teacher with a horse's tail and a bright red dress. The torrent passed. The Englishwoman came in and paid for her ticket. She stepped beneath a strip of fluorescent lighting

and for the first time Rollison was able to study her closely,
for she stood looking round for him while he hid behind a
statue dug up by zealots from the wastes of Babylon.
Obviously she was looking for him. Until now, he had
judged that she was in the late twenties; now, he thought,
she was probably nearer forty, but a superbly preserved
forty; only the suspicion of lines at her eyes as well as her
expression gave her away.

Her disappointment was all too obvious.

Rollison stepped from behind the ancient statue, and
pretending not to notice her, strolled along the wide corri-
dors past ancient relics of pots and pans and other impedi-
menta, tools of the housewives of many centuries ago.
Leading off were several recesses which were not likely to
be frequented by the horde of school children or by anyone but a specialist. Rollison appeared to study a piece of
Assyrian pottery so perfectly stuck together that it was
hard to believe the legend on the label near it; it had been
found in seventy-two different pieces by Professor le Fevre.
Who, wondered Rollison vaguely, was Professor le Fevre?
He felt that shiver of doubt and guilt which comes to all
when in the presence of antiquity they should know about
but do not.

The Englishwoman was coming nearer.

No one else was in this recess, and it was ten or twelve
feet from the main passage. Footsteps echoed, quite
faintly. A gallery attendant passed, jingling some keys.
Rollison now turned and faced the woman, and smiled
tentatively.

"At least it's pleasantly cool in here," he said.

"Yes, isn't it?" she agreed, and he fancied that she caught
her breath. "Are you—you *are* Mr. Rollison, aren't you?"

"Yes."

"Mr.—the Honourable *Richard* Rollison."

He smiled more broadly.

"Yes."

"Sometimes called—" she hesitated, and then the word came out with a rush: "—the Toff."

"Ridiculous, isn't it?" asked Rollison. "I once made the mistake of parading round the East End of London late at night with a bevy of lovelies and an opera hat, and the name has stuck ever since."

She didn't smile, and yet he had a feeling that she would look lovely if she did. He studied her closely, without appearing to be too bold. Feature by feature or simply as a face on its own, hers was quite lovely. Her eyes had a curious honey brown colour, not tawny but clear as honey fresh from the comb. Her upper lip was perhaps a trifle short, her nose was a trifle *rétroussé*. This gave her an expression almost of wonderment, as if she didn't quite believe all that she saw. She had a nicely rounded chin, and a slender, golden tanned neck. The linen suit was supremely cut, and cunningly too; it concealed the depth of her bosom and accentuated the trimness of her waist.

"How can I help you?" Rollison asked at last.

She said, very quickly, almost nervously: "I don't really know. Can you spare a little time so that we—we can talk in private?"

"Gladly."

"You're very kind. Where—where do you think would be a good place?"

"We could go and have tea in the Bois de Boulogne, or one of a dozen places where—"

"I want to be sure that we can't be overheard."

"Your hotel, then?" Rollison suggested.

She said, uneasily: "Could we—could we go to your hotel room?"

"Of course," agreed Rollison, and did not ask her why. "We'll get a taxi, I'm at the George V."

"No, please," the Englishwoman said. "I'll be at your hotel in half an hour's time, and will telephone you as soon as I arrive. Thank you—thank you very much indeed." She turned and began to hurry away, and again Rollison was struck by the slender beauty of her legs and the way she carried herself, but he was much more intrigued by her manner and her tactics. Was she as nervous as she made out? If she were, two possible explanations were at hand: first, that she was frightened in case they were seen together; second, that she was going to ask far more of him than she should. At the back of his mind too, there was another possibility which he did not want to acknowledge, but which was inescapably there.

She might be trying to make a monkey out of him.

She might, for instance, be hoping to borrow money, and be putting on this act of embarrassment to soften him up. She might even be planning to take him for a ride. Nice, virtuous, self-respecting Englishwomen did not commonly arrange to meet a strange man in his hotel room. The possibilities of having been selected as a prince of suckers could not be ignored.

Certainly there was something peculiar about her tension, about the way she had followed him, about the way she had spoken; and it was significant that she had not given him a name, either real or false. With admirable detachment he considered that once in his room, she would tear off her clothes and threaten to scream unless he paid for her silence. He grinned; if she did he had made the mistake of his life.

It was now nearly half-past twelve and he would get the visit from the police at three o'clock, so if this were a simple appeal for help he could hear the story, have lunch with the lady, and give himself time to think about it while making his formal complaint over the loss of his wallet. He felt it possible that the unknown woman had some genuine need for his help and was not seriously worried, but he wished he knew why the little man had followed her. Forgetting the forged money and allowing his imagination to run riot, it was conceivable that the man had been a kind of keeper, and that the woman was a mental case.

When Rollison reached the road running across the end of the Louvre again, he saw the woman getting into a taxi. No one appeared to take any interest in her, certainly no one followed her. He took another taxi, and was at his hotel, near the Champs Elysées, at ten minutes to one. The hotel was select, quiet, and something of a club for knowing English and American patrons. Georges, the six-foot commissionaire, M. Forelle, the rotund Assistant Manager, Albert the tiny lift boy in his puce uniform and rows of silver buttons, all greeted him as an old friend. There was no sign of the Englishwoman. He was whisked up to the sixth floor in the only hotel elevator in Paris which rose swiftly. Albert beamed farewell and slammed the doors, and Rollison strolled to the end of the corridor, his footsteps muffled by the thick pile carpet. A window there overlooked the Arc de Triomphe and the lunatic bedlam of the road around it; so did one of the windows of his room, which was on a corner; the other was overlooking the Champs Elysées and the chestnut trees. He was often in a mood, now, when he could sit on his tiny balcony, look at the scene, and enjoy it, while being glad that most of the noise had faded by the time it reached this height.

He opened his door, and glanced at the keyhole and the escutcheon plate. On this bright brass plate, he saw some scratches.

For a second, no more, he stood quite still, key in the lock, studying the scratches. They were bright and freshly made, very close to the keyhole, and almost certainly the result of someone using a key carelessly—possibly a skeleton key. No member of the hotel staff was likely to use a master key like that; they all seemed to find the keyhole by a kind of sleight of hand.

He turned the key and pushed the door open, slowly at first. He saw no cause for alarm, although an imitation Louis Quinze mirror, beautifully framed in gilt, showed him the reflection of most of the room and also the door. No one stood behind it. He pushed it open more briskly, and began to hum to himself.

The room was empty.

It was very small, hardly worthy of the title sitting-room, yet it had two armchairs and a couch and a table all in a fair reproduction of Louis Quinze. The bedroom much larger, lay beyond the bathroom, which led off to the right. Rollison still hummed to himself as he passed the bathroom door, opened it and glanced inside. Then he stepped in, turned on the taps, waited for half a minute and pressed the button which worked the flush. Under cover of these noises he stepped to the door of the bedroom, half prepared to find someone approaching him with a weapon in his hand.

No one came.

The bedroom, large and graceful, with powder blue walls and a hint of Wedgwood about the ceiling and the décor, was also empty.

As he hummed, he reflected: "I could be making a thorough fool of myself." He looked round, studying the bed, the carpet, the position of the personal oddments on the dressing-table, everything; and he noticed nothing unusual. The windows leading to the balcony were closed but the shutters were not up; the maid had learned that he liked the brightness of the sun in his room and preferred not to live in a state of perpetual gloom. He stepped to the balcony. If anyone stood out there, hiding, their movement would be restricted and he had little to fear.

He pressed close against the glass of the doors and could see most of the balcony; no one was there.

"In fact I *am* making a fool of myself," he declared aloud, and just to make sure that no one was pressing close against the corner between the balcony and the wall, he opened the windows. His chair was in its usual position; an ashtray he had used that morning had been cleaned but was back in its place on a small metal table. He drew back, and then bent down and lifted the drape at the side of the bed; no one was underneath.

He grinned, and remarked aloud:

"I'm putting up quite a performance this morning, aren't I?" He glanced at his watch; it was then ten minutes before the unknown Englishwoman was due. He stood in the middle of the room and scrutinised every piece of furniture, every part of the wall, the two Renoir prints which weren't at all bad, the table by the side of the bed, the reading lamp, the telephone, the—

He stopped smiling.

He went forward and bent down near that bedside table, closer than he had on the first scrutiny. There were three wires where two should be. Apart from the telephone cable, thick and black and obvious, and the lamp flex, a silver-coloured wire led from the plug adaptor on the wainscotting behind the table. He moved the table and examined the adaptor and plug; both had been wiped clean, presumably to remove prints. He traced the silver wire up behind the bedpost, and fastened to the back of the bed, which was satin upon metal, was a small tape recorder. This was so tiny that when the lid was closed it was little larger than a pocket book, although fatter; it would slip easily into a man's pocket or a woman's handbag.

"It's nice to know that I'm not in my dotage yet," he said aloud. "Now I wonder why all this——" his voice trailed off. He pulled the bed a little further from the wall, and studied the machine. It was plugged straight into the adaptor and should be working; why wasn't it? Did it have to be switched on? When the Englishwoman came, would she know it was there and find some way of operating it? He contemplated the machine—and then quite suddenly he raised his voice and said: "*I just don't know*" in a firm, clear voice; immediately the wheels began to revolve. "So that's it," he mused. "Sensitive to volume, it starts whenever people start talking." He stopped, and the machine went on; he watched it for fully a minute before the wheels ceased turning. "That patent should be worth quite a fortune," he observed softly, and walked away from the machine pushing the bed a little closer to the wall, and went on: "But what's it all about? Is she going to do a strip-tease act and then start the spiel to be used in evidence later?" He did not like to think that of the Englishwoman, but only a fool would fail to consider the possibility.

He glanced at his watch; it was precisely twenty-nine minutes since the woman had said she would see him here in half an hour; and as he lowered his arm, the telephone bell rang.

He went across, lifted it, pressed his head against the wall and realised that the bell had started the tape recorder, so everything would go on record.

"Richard Rollison here," he said.

"May I come up?" asked the woman who had followed him.

3

CAUSE FOR FEAR?

SHE came in swiftly, and seemed relieved when Rollison closed the door. He said: "I'll lead the way, shall I?" and went through the little ante-room into the bedroom. He should soon know if this were to be one of the oldest attempts at blackmail known to man. She hardly glanced about the room, certainly did not look towards the head of the bed as if she were aware of what was hidden there. The sound of traffic from the Place de L'Etoile hummed clearly but made only a background, and did not threaten to make talking difficult. The woman glanced out at the beautiful blue of the sky, then turned to face him; Rollison had the impression that she had screwed herself up for this, that all she wanted to say would soon come tumbling out.

"Mr. Rollison, I've no possible excuse for harassing you in this way," she began, "but I'm so worried I hardly know what to do. I don't sleep well, I can't eat, I—I'm afraid I'll become a nervous wreck if this goes on any longer."

She paused for a moment, but he thought it wiser not to interrupt.

"I tried to see you in London, I telephoned your flat three times, and then learned from a newspaper paragraph that you were in Paris. It—it made little difference whether I saw you in London or here—in fact, it might be better here—and I simply had to talk to someone. Even if you can't help I know you're absolutely trustworthy and won't betray my confidence. You won't, will you?"

"No," said Rollison.

"You don't know me at all, but we have a mutual friend in Lady Bennet, and I met Lady Gloria Hurst, your aunt, a few weeks ago. This trouble hadn't started then. Had it started, I would probably have talked to Lady Gloria, she seemed so completely competent. But I understand that she is in Italy now."

"She is," said Rollison. As an introduction, talk of Helena Bennet and of his Aunt Gloria could hardly be bettered. The idea of a strip-tease was fading fast. "And you never know, I may be able to help," he added.

"Oh, *God*, I hope you can!" the woman cried, and to prove how distraught she was, she pushed her hat back from her forehead, a little net of flowers which had looked so becoming; she snatched it off and poked her fingers through silky feathery hair which was the same colour as her eyes. Now Rollison saw that those eyes were too bright, something had given her a headache since he had last seen her. "Mr. Rollison," she announced, "my husband has disappeared."

Rollison said: "*I see*," in a tone which seemed to suggest that she had explained everything, whereas in fact she had explained only one thing: it was almost certain that he could not help her. Errant and erring husbands were not his cup of tea. Not very long ago, however, another woman had come to him at his Mayfair flat making just such a statement: that her husband had disappeared. He had felt the sinking of his heart then, feeling sure that the wife had really wanted a private detective with a keyhole-and-back-door technique; but that case had not been all it seemed. Would this? Certainly he must be very careful not to encourage this woman to think that he would help if it were a simple matter of husband-chasing. His reputation for detection made some people think that he simply plied for hire.

The woman was looking at him expectantly; the "I *see*," hadn't been quite enough.

"And when did this happen?" he asked.

"On April the first," she answered. "Actually on All Fools' Day." She raised her white, slim hands, which were clenched tightly, and for a moment he thought that she was going to burst into tears. She did not. She dropped her arms by her side and went on much more calmly: "I don't want to behave emotionally, Mr. Rollison. When I look back, I can hardly believe that I have behaved the way I have during the past seven weeks, but—anxiety and fear soon rub the veneer of composure off, don't they?"

She said that very quietly; tensely.

"Meaning we're all much the same underneath," Rollison said. "I couldn't agree more. Come and sit down and have a drink—I can run to a gin and Italian, French or bitter lemon, whisky and soda, or Dubonnet."

"I think I'll have a Dubonnet," she said, and watched him as he opened a small walnut cabinet and poured the drinks, a whisky and soda for himself. He carried another chair on to the balcony, where a gentle breeze blew her hair. Without the little hat she was slightly less sleek, and looked a little younger, as if the girl of twenty years ago was not really lost completely. She took her drink, and said: "When it first happened I thought it was a kind of joke." She stared at Rollison, holding her glass poised. "What would *you* think if someone telephoned you on the first of April, at about eleven o'clock in the morning, and said that your husband was going away, there was no need to expect him home tonight?"

"April fool," said Rollison.

"Exactly! That's what I thought too, I laughed, and said that I wasn't fooled as easily as that, and rang off. A few minutes afterwards the man telephoned again and said that he wasn't fooling—then *he* rang off. It worried me, rather, and I telephoned my husband's office."

She was telling the story very well, it was even possible to believe that her pauses were carefully timed.

"His secretary said that he had left about ten o'clock and hadn't said when he was coming back," his visitor went on. "That jolted me badly. I can remember it so vividly, sometimes I seem to hear her speaking to me. 'I'm sorry, Mrs. Dangerfield, but Mr. Dangerfield went out just after ten o'clock and didn't say when he would be back. I rather thought that he was going to meet you.' "

The words trailed off.

"Do you know why his secretary said that?" asked Rollison.

"Well, not really, although in a way I suppose I do," said Mrs. Dangerfield; she had brought in her name very naturally. "My husband really had only two interests, Mr. Rollison—his home and his office. I've talked to Betty—Miss Oliver, his secretary—about it, several times. She said that he didn't give her any reason to think that he was coming to see me, but she rather took it for granted. Now and again we would meet in mid-morning and do some shopping at Harrods, and have lunch together. Usually Alec would tell Betty what he was going to do, but not always. He—he's always been a little absent-minded."

"What does he do for a living?" inquired Rollison.

"He has an art agency, rather a specialised one." Mrs. Dangerfield hesitated, sipped her drink, and went on: "I mean, he represents a number of commercial artists and photographers, sells their work and gets commissions for them. It's a highly specialised business, but I think I ought to say that he doesn't really do it for a living. He has ample independent means. We both have, if it comes to that. But Alec couldn't just drift or have a good time, and he's always been interested in art, the commercial side of art chiefly. He isn't an intellectual or a modernist, he—" she hesitated, and then for the first time smiled; she had beautiful teeth, and the smile made her look younger and almost gay. "He's a perfectly normal individual, Mr. Rollison—not at all arty. In fact he abominates artiness and Bohemianism, and gets almost apoplectic about some of the so-called action painters."

"Ah," said Rollison, non-committally.

"I'm trying to give you an idea of what he's like," explained Mrs. Dangerfield. Her smile disappeared and tension came back; but the drink, the naturalness of the situation, the wind blowing gently through her hair, the beautiful cloudless sky and the loveliness of the white-flowered trees in the wide thoroughfare below all helped her. "We've been married for twenty years, and I am quite sure that I know Alec as well as it's possible to know another person. We are seldom apart. Now and again he has to go to Paris or Florence, or Amsterdam perhaps, and even to New York, to see artists and other artist's agents and their customers. Usually I go with him. We are very close indeed, and—I am *quite* sure that he is in love with me, Mr. Rollison."

Rollison thought: "Now she's coming to the other woman."

"And I am as sure as I can be that there isn't another woman," declared Mrs. Dangerfield decisively. "I know that the wife is supposed to be the last person to know if her husband is having an *affaire*, but—well, unless I had incontrovertible evidence, I simply wouldn't believe that Alec is having one. Besides, it's so—" she broke off.

Rollison finished his whisky reflectively. The more she talked the more he liked her. She had a clear mind and a straightforward approach, but that anxiety showed through all the time. As he watched her, studying the rather too bright eyes, the beautifully clear skin and the clean-cut features, he came to the conclusion that few men would have an *affaire* if they had a wife as lovely as she, and one as intelligent as she seemed to be.

"Haven't you heard from him since he disappeared?" he asked, more briskly.

She looked at him uncertainly and answered unexpectedly: "I don't know."

Rollison seemed startled.

"I realise that sounds quite absurd, but it's the truth," she insisted, and closed her eyes for a moment, then put her glass down and stood up. She went close to the railings and stood with the breeze blowing her hair off her forehead, stirring the open jacket of her suit, rustling her skirt. "Someone who *says* that he's Alec telephones me from time to time." She stared across the rooftops of Paris. "Sometimes I think it is his voice, sometimes I think it's someone mimicking it. The message is always the same. I'm not to worry, he will be back one day. And I am not to go to the police, I am not to go to anyone for help." Now she turned and looked down at Rollison, and went on: "I was terrified of coming to see you, in case it would do him any harm. You see, I once—I once went to a small detective agency, in Chancery Lane. A friend of mine had been divorced, so she knew about this agency, and I went to see if they could help. I didn't like the man I saw, he seemed absolutely sure that he had to look for another woman, so I didn't go any further with him. In any case—" she hesitated, closed her eyes again, and then said in a high-pitched voice: "I was telephoned the next

day and told that if I went to anyone else for help, I would
never see Alec again. I couldn't bring myself to try again,
and so waited for six weeks. Most weeks I had a telephone
call from Alec, or someone who pretended to be Alec. He
didn't really talk like Alec, didn't use the same kind of
words and phrases, but it sounded very like his voice.
I simply couldn't stand it any more. I telephoned you, and
when I discovered you were in Paris I thought it would
probably be safer to talk to you here. That's why I
wouldn't go to a restaurant, why I had to see you—well,
I suppose furtively is the word. I'm afraid of being found
out, afraid that something I do might harm Alec, yet I
simply can't stand the strain of not knowing the truth any
longer."

"I can understand that very well," Rollison said. "I
don't think you need worry, Mrs. Dangerfield."

She looked at him very straightly, and there was a
sterner note in her voice when she spoke again. Rollison
had a feeling that something unexpected was coming, but
wasn't prepared for her to say:

"Mr. Rollison, I hope you won't try to reassure me by
platitudinous remarks. Of course there is reason to worry.
I am almost distraught with anxiety, and until I know the
truth about Alec I am likely to be. You may not realise
how difficult it is for me to talk as calmly as I am doing
now. There are times when I could burst into tears, other
times when I feel that I could scream at the top of my
voice. You—you have such a remarkable reputation that
I thought you might possibly be able to help me, but I
would much rather you told me if you can't or if you won't.
And I would much prefer it if you didn't talk in plati-
tudes."

By the time she finished, Rollison was chuckling.

"Nicely put," he said warmly, "and I won't be any

more prosy than I can help." He stood up, and leaned against the railing, oblivious of the sheer drop of over a hundred feet to the pavement below. "I didn't mean that you had no cause to worry, simply that there was no need to worry about harming your husband as a result of this meeting."

"You can only guess—"

"Not really," Rollison protested, and told her about the little man who had followed her, the wallet trick, and the fact that the man certainly could not report that she had met him.

"I see what you mean," said Mrs. Dangerfield. "But sooner or later you will have to make the statement to the courts, and it's possible that the people behind it all will think you accused the man because you were already trying to help me. Surely that's obvious?" She stopped on an accusing note.

She had a good mind; and she could not have said more clearly that she feared that Rollison might have done more harm than good.

4

DEGREE OF RISK

"Well, it *is* possible that they take it for granted that I've asked you for help, isn't it?" asked Mrs. Dangerfield.

"Yes," agreed Rollison.

"I'm not blaming you—" she began.

"Nice of you," Rollison interrupted, "but if you'd telephoned and told me part of this you could have made quite sure that no alarm was raised."

"I've told you, I tried to in London," she said, "and I didn't know where you were in Paris. I've haunted places like the Opera and the Café de Paris in the hope of seeing you, and today—" she broke off, and then added bitterly: "What you're really saying is that it's my fault?"

"I mean, it's happened and I'm not sure that it's a bad thing," said Rollison, and held up his hand as she was about to interrupt. "No, I am not trying to blarney you, I'm quite serious." He spread out his arms and gripped the railing as he looked at her; he liked everything that he saw, even the uncertainty in her eyes. "Is this your first encounter with crime?"

"Yes. If it *is* crime."

"It's crime of a kind," Rollison assured her. "And whoever is responsible is very anxious to keep you away from the police or from anyone who might be able to help you. If he weren't nervous because they might interfere with his plans, he wouldn't take the trouble. The 'don't-go-to-the-police-or-else' gambit could mean a case of jitters.

34

Do you know what I would do next time you have a message?"

She said slowly: "I think I can guess. You'd tell this man that I've asked for your help."

"That's exactly what I would do," asserted Rollison. He heard a faint noise, above them, and was puzzled; and he put his head on one side as he appraised her, so that he could look up. She went straight to the point always—and he wondered whether she had heard the noise too.

He caught a glimpse of something dark jutting out from the roof; it wasn't a slate but a piece of masonry. The faint scraping sound came again, and he glanced up and saw that the piece of stone was an inch or two further over the edge than it had been a moment before. A faint powdering of dust lazed in the air, too. Was it sliding or being pushed? Mrs. Dangerfield glanced up, opened her mouth to cry out, and bit her lips when he raised his hand hastily.

"Are you prepared to take some risk?" he asked in a normal tone of voice. When she didn't answer, but stared fixedly upwards, he went on: "You won't have much success if you're not." He mouthed: "*Answer me.*" She saw the way his lips moved, gulped, and said:

"It—it depends how great the risk is."

"I don't think it's very great," Rollison told her, and gripped the railing more tightly, looking up fascinated as the stone edged nearer and nearer. It was swaying. In a moment it would fall. Had he not noticed it in time it would almost certainly have struck him on the head, might even have toppled him over to the pavement below. "It's now nearly seven weeks since you've seen your husband, and you can't be sure whether he's alive or dead. You can't even be sure that—"

The stone tipped over.

It loomed above Rollison like a great boulder, looking much larger than it was, and blotting out the sky. He dodged to one side, stretched out his arms, let the stone fall against his hands and heaved it inwards from the balcony. The weight and pressure against his arms was agonising, but instead of striking the rail and falling downwards, it crashed down on to the balcony and did no harm. As it fell thundering, he said urgently to Mrs. Dangerfield:

"Go inside, lock the doors, don't open them until you hear my voice."

He swung round from her, hearing her cry: "*Where are you going?*" but ignored her.

There were balconies like his all along this side of the hotel, and it was not the first time he had leapt across so wide a gap. He climbed on to the railing, stretched upwards, found that he could touch the guttering, but just here it was broken by the stone. He jumped down, then put his hands on the side of the railing and leapt to the one in the next room. He caught a glimpse of a fat woman, sitting at a dressing-table, clad in a brassière and a pair of panties. She screamed as she stared at him; he just heard the sound. He stretched up, clutched the guttering, and hauled himself up and over. He knew that if the man who had moved that stone was on the roof waiting for him, he would have little chance, but some risks had to be taken.

The roof was nearly flat; and a man was dodging behind a chimney breast.

Rollison hauled himself up and over. He stood crouching, then ran crabwise along the roof towards the chimney breast. He heard a bang, as of a door being closed, rounded the chimneys and saw a big glass roof-light just ahead of him. He jumped towards it. Beneath him a man was stretched up, obviously trying to shoot the bolt of the frame. Rollison stamped on a pane of glass. It splintered, and showered down on the man, who snatched his hand away and turned towards a narrow flight of stairs. Rollison got a grip on the edge of the roof-light, hauled, and found that it came up without much trouble. He let it crash back. The man disappeared round a bend of the stairs. Rollison raced down the stairs, if the other had been armed he would have used his weapon by now; yet Rollison steadied as he reached the corner, flattened himself against it, and peered round.

Just round the corner, also flat against the wall, and with a flick knife in his hand, was the man he was chasing. He seemed to be taken completely off his balance, gave a gasping cry, leapt at Rollison, striking out with the knife. Its point caught Rollison's coat then scraped along the wall. Before the man could strike again, Rollison went for him, kicking at the hand which held the knife.

The man backed away, clutching the knife; and Rollison's foot caught him in the stomach. He staggered away. Rollison went after him, grappled, caught his wrist and twisted: and the knife dropped. He was breathing very hard as the other tried to tear himself free, tried to kick out, but missed by inches. Rollison twisted the thick, bony wrist, felt the arm turning, heard the man's gasping, knew that the arm could not stand much more pressure.

The man squealed; and stopped struggling.

"That's better," Rollison said, and let him go, then grabbed his shoulder and twisted him round, took the wrist again and forced it up in a hammerlock. "Forward," he ordered in English, and the man began to move forward, unable to refuse.

At the foot of this flight of stairs was a small door, marked *Exit*. Forcing the man to one side, he pulled at the handle, and the door opened slowly. It was of steel, and fireproof. It opened on to a carpeted passage, and Rollison pushed his victim through. For a few seconds they were in the passage leading to his room, and any one of the doors might open. The lift was humming. Rollison reached his own door, tapped sharply, and called:

"It's all right." He fumbled for his key, but before he could get it out, the door opened and Mrs. Dangerfield stood holding the door with her left hand, the other raised to her lips.

"Hallo," Rollison said briskly, and smiled. He thrust the man forward as the woman darted to one side, slipped in, and closed the door. "First move is over," he went on, and he was almost breathless, as he asked: "Do you know this joker?"

She was staring at the man.

"No," she said, quite steadily. "No, I've never seen him before."

"Probably not your loss," said Rollison. He needed time to recover from the fierce exertion and the shock of the narrow escape, and he made that time by speaking in jerky sentences, and doing everything with slow deliberation. He frogmarched his captive into the bedroom, and Mrs. Dangerfield hovered close behind him. "Push that small chair against the wall by the bathroom door, please," asked Rollison, and when she had done so, he let his prisoner go, twisted him round at the shoulders, and thrust him down on to the chair; the man put up no kind of fight. "This is Menace Number 2," declared Rollison, standing back and studying the prisoner closely. "Menace Number one is in a police cell, or wherever the French put their rogues." He took out cigarettes, lit one, and was keenly aware of Mrs. Dangerfield's gaze.

The man was staring, too.

He had not uttered a word and he had not made any attempt to get away, yet his expression betrayed how frightened he was. Moreover, an air about him made one thing clear; he was English. The cut of his clothes and his shoes, the cut of his features, even the cut of his hair, all showed that. He was in the late twenties, had crisp, wiry fair hair, a healthy tan, very clear blue eyes. In all other circumstances Rollison would have felt that he was a healthy games-loving decent chap, as school tie English as a man could be, probably lacking in imagination but certainly filled to the brim with traditional notions of fair play. Rollison would bet a small fortune that the man had learned whatever he knew at a minor Public School.

"Who *is* he?" demanded Mrs. Dangerfield.

"We're about to find out," Rollison told her. "Would you care to pour me out a whisky and soda? And one for him?"

"For h—" she began, and then turned away, as if she realised that it would be pointless to ask questions or question his wisdom. Whisky gurgled, soda splashed, the prisoner moistened his lips and looked bewildered. Mrs. Dangerfield brought the drinks, handed Rollison his first, then put a glass into the other man's hand.

"Thanks," he muttered and tossed the whisky down. Rollison sipped.

"Name, address, occupation," he inquired.

"It—it's no use asking me to say anything, I'm not going to," the prisoner said; his voice was that of an educated man. "Nothing you can do will make me."

Rollison, feeling much better, beamed at Mrs. Dangerfield.

"He has a lot to learn, hasn't he?" He motioned carelessly to the captive. "See what he has in his coat pockets, will you?" He winked without the prisoner noticing, and

Mrs. Dangerfield went forward. She was remarkable in many ways, not least her quickness on the uptake. The prisoner tried to move back, but only succeeded in banging his head on the wall. Mrs. Dangerfield took the front of his coat and held it open, and made as if to put her right hand in the inside pocket. He pushed her hand away. As he did so, Rollison flashed forward, slapped him half a dozen times on either cheek, sharp, resounding blows which rocked him right and left; then Rollison drew back, and waited until the man had recovered a little, although his cheeks were still flaming under the impact of those blows.

At last Rollison said: "Never strike the weaker sex. You should have learned that years ago."

The man moistened his lips again.

"Now let's see—" began Rollison, and went forward, but before he reached the man, Mrs. Dangerfield interrupted:

"No, let me."

Rollison stood aside. She went close to the prisoner, opened his coat, and this time took out a wallet without any interference. She handed this to Rollison, then felt in the side pockets of the coat, drew out a folded handkerchief, a comb, a gold cigarette case, a gold cigarette lighter, and two paper bus tickets. She handed these to Rollison one after the other, then said to the man:

"Stand up, please."

Rollison gulped at the "please."

"Don't make any more difficulties," Mrs. Dangerfield ordered sharply.

Perhaps it was the look in Rollison's eyes rather than the tone of her voice which made the prisoner stand up hurriedly. With complete *sangfroid*, Mrs. Dangerfield slipped her hands into his trousers pockets, drew out a small handful of coins, a key, and a fold of paper money from the hip pocket. Then she slapped the pockets lightly, and said:

"I think that's everything."

"What a policewoman you'd make," said Rollison feelingly. "Would you like to have first go at the wallet?"

"You won't find anything there," the Englishman declared. "It's a waste of time."

"What makes you so sure?" inquired Rollison.

"I made sure nothing could go wrong, so everything I've got on is new. Rollison, if you don't let me go you'll regret it. You don't know what you are doing, it's madness to—"

He broke off, Mrs. Dangerfield swung round, and Rollison raised his head sharply, for there was a loud banging at the door of the apartment.

5

INITIALS S.R.S.

"WHAT's that?" the man exclaimed, and jumped to his feet; what little colour he had had drained away.

"Perhaps your friends have come to rescue you," suggested Rollison dryly. "More likely someone heard the row when that piece of rock fell, and reported it. Sit down, and try to look as if you're a welcome guest." He moved into the ante-room as another loud knock came. He opened the door, standing so that no one could push past him. He was not all surprised to see two men and one fat woman, the woman now wearing a dress. The taller of the two men said:

"There is a thief in the hotel, M'sieu. This lady saw him. Did you see him, please?"

"Thief?" echoed Rollison, with convincing astonishment. "Good lord, no. I've friends here for a drink, and we heard nothing." His fluent French would almost certainly have astounded the Yorkshireman and the gendarme of the Rue de Rivoli. "I say," he said, and looked back into the room, "you two heard nothing, did you?"

He half expected the fat woman from next door to identify him, but she did not. The two men came in, one of them the Assistant Manager's Assistant, another the house detective, but the visit was a formality, more than a search, and they stayed only for half a minute. Rollison earnestly wished them luck and hoped that no one had suffered any severe loss, then closed the door on them. He picked up his glass, finished his drink, wiped a film of perspiration off his forehead, and said to the prisoner:

"Before we're through you'll probably wish you'd been safely lodged in the Bastille." He went to the telephone and the prisoner stared at him, catching his breath when Rollison asked for a call to London, and cried out when he gave the number—Whitehall 1212.

"You can't do that! If you do, Dangerfield will—" He broke off.

"Mr. Rollison," said Mrs. Dangerfield, in a rather stilted voice, "I must ask you to do nothing which might worsen the situation for my husband."

"You can't really have it all your own way," said Rollison reasoningly. "This chap nearly cracked my skull, would have cheerfully knocked me off the balcony to become a mess of pulp on the pavement, was ready to slice me up with a knife when I went after him. I take a dim view of all of it, and it's now a personal issue." Again he fluttered an eyelid at the woman, then examined all the oddments which he had dropped on to the bed. There was nothing in the wallet to give the man away; no driving licence, no letters—in fact the wallet was empty except for some English money and a book of English postage stamps. The only clue of any kind were the bus tickets—a Numero 87 bus. The fact that there were two of them might mean that the man had made the same journey twice; the numbers weren't consecutive, as they would have been had two travelled at the same time.

Rollison went to the telephone again, called the dining-room, and said: "Pierre, will you keep me a quiet table for two, I'll be down as soon as I can." When the Head Waiter promised that he should have the best table in the restaurant, he rang off, glanced at his watch, and saw that it was twenty minutes past one. "About three o'clock the police are coming to have a chat with me about the pick-pocket in the Rue de Rivoli; so we mustn't be long, must we?"

He lit a cigarette, picked up the gold cigarette case and studied it closely. "I don't know whether you'd like to powder your nose," he suggested to Mrs. Dangerfield, "but once the London call's come through, I think we ought to go and eat."

"What about him?"

"He can starve."

"You can't leave him here without anyone to guard him!"

"I shouldn't worry about that," Rollison said. "He won't be able to get far if we make a good job of tying him up." He beamed, as the man's breath hissed and Mrs. Dangerfield put her head on one side, as if she were finding all this hard to understand. She picked up her handbag and went into the bathroom, and had been there for three or four minutes when the telephone bell rang. As Rollison lifted it, she appeared in the bathroom doorway. A hair-pin was between her lips, and a comb in her hand; she was not going to miss a trick.

"Scotland Yard . . ." Rollison said. "Fine . . . It's Richard Rollison here . . . Yes, all the way from Paris! . . . Yes, if he's in . . . Thanks." There was a pause, before he asked casually: "What's the weather like over there? . . . Oh, too bad . . . Quite beautiful here, and Paris is such a surprising city . . . Oh, I only want some information about a bad man . . ." His tone changed, and he spoke more crisply: "Hallo, Bill, having a sand-wich instead of a square meal? . . . Just to make you envious, I'm about to eat at one of the best restaurants in Paris . . . Yes . . . Well, it's really a simple matter. I want to trace a chap you might have on your books. His initials are S.R.S.—S for Stanley, R for Robert, S for Stanley. Twenty-eight or nine, five feet eleven, fair-haired, pale blue eyes, slight scar on right side of chin, tailored by Meldrum of Savile Row, shoes by Abbling of Bury Street, man-about-townish . . . Well, the quicker the better, can you give me a call this afternoon? I'm at . . ." he gave the hotel number, said 'thanks' warmly, and rang off. "That shouldn't take very long," he said, and studied the face of the man whose initials were S.R.S.

The prisoner was appalled.

"So you have a record," Rollison remarked with satisfaction. "The public schoolboy gone to the devil is the easiest man to trace, didn't you know that?" He was aware of Mrs. Dangerfield staring intently and for the first time the edge of doubt seemed to have been removed from her expression; she smiled as she went back into the bathroom.

"Rollison, this won't do you any good," S.R.S. muttered. "You may think you're being clever, but if you don't let me go, she'll never see her husband again. That's as true as I'm sitting here. If you let me go——"

"Not a hope," said Rollison, and added musingly, "Yet. Ever seen one of these?" He held out his hand, the fingers open, towards S.R.S. who glanced down. Rollison doubled his fist and struck the man sharply on the side of the chin: and his victim gave a gasp of sound, and lolled back against the wall. "Probably no hope at all," he added briskly. He went to the wall, removed the tape recorder from its position, tugging at the flex; it came out of the adaptor easily. He took out a knife which had several all-purpose blades including a pair of wire cutters, snipped the flex so that he had two pieces of equal length, first bound the man's wrists behind him, then his ankles. When he finished he turned round, and was not surprised

to see Mrs. Dangerfield watching him. She was immaculate again, and wearing her hat.

"Bring me the roll of adhesive tape out of my washbag,
will you?" asked Rollison. She turned away immediately,
and not only brought the tape but a pair of nail scissors.
She was already pulling the tape off the roll.

"How much do you need?" she asked.

"Two pieces of five or six inches each."

She snipped.

"Thanks," said Rollison.

"Shouldn't you warm it, to make sure it sticks well?"
asked Mrs. Dangerfield.

"Not this kind," Rollison assured her. He pulled the
man's head up, and Mrs. Dangerfield moved to one side,
placed a hand at each of the man's temples, and watched
as Rollison pressed the adhesive tape over the full lips,
making sure that S.R.S. could not call out.

"Fine," said Rollison. "Now we'll roll him under the
bed." He lifted the man to his feet as Mrs. Dangerfield
pulled back the bedspread; then lowered him and pushed
him under. When Rollison straightened out and dusted
his hands, he was smiling at her. It was as if the man with
the initials S.R.S. had been rolled out of existence. "I
could work with you for a long time," he remarked to
Mrs. Dangerfield. "Ready for food?"

"I *am* rather hungry," Mrs. Dangerfield said and
marvelled. "Yet I haven't really felt like eating for
weeks."

"It's the excitement," declared Rollison, "and the fact
that you're no longer in this alone. A trouble halved is a
troubled shared, don't the cliché makers say?"

"It's the other way round."

"So it is! I'll just wash my hands." Rollison went into
the bathroom, and when he came out saw her in the door-

way leading to the balcony, staring down at the stone. She joined him and said almost musingly:

"That would have killed you."

"I suppose it might have," agreed Rollison, "but I hope it was meant to scare rather than kill. Old S.R.S. couldn't have reckoned on me standing in a position where I'd get it bang on the boko. They're a very lively mob."

"I ought to feel more frightened," said Mrs. Dangerfield, "but for some reason, I don't."

"You're beginning to think about this instead of simply feeling about it," said Rollison. "Now, let's forget it until we're downstairs. Pierre will have a table in a corner, and we'll be able to talk without being overheard. I want to know everything you can possibly tell me."

Before she could say a word, the lift came up. Young Albert greeted them with a bright smile, and they were whisked downstairs. The small restaurant overlooked the Champs Elysées from the first floor, and the immediate impression it created was exactly right; most of the tables were occupied, more than half of the occupants were French, waiters were busy with their methylated spirit stoves, there was a murmur of conversation, and Pierre, who looked slightly like Maurice Chevalier, was waiting for them. On his advice they ordered *truite au beurre* to be followed by a *specialité de la maison*: "Veal, with a leetle egg, a leetle crust around it, a leetle sauce . . . *superb*." Pierre kissed his fingers.

The *specialité* was superb.

It was ten minutes to three, and Rollison was allowing himself three more minutes here when a waiter came up to say:

"A telephone call for you, M'sieu, from London."

"London!" ejaculated Mrs. Dangerfield. "Already!"

"I'll come," said Rollison, and added to the waiter, "If

anyone calls to see me, keep them downstairs until I'm ready, will you?"

He went to the telephone booth near the dining-room, knowing that the woman was hating the fact that she could not hear what he was saying.

It was Superintendent Grice of New Scotland Yard.

"I don't know what you've found over in Paris, Rolly, but I want to very soon," he said. "The man you're interested in is almost certainly Simon Roy Shawn. He's an artist, particularly good at engraving, and he went down for three years for being not quite good enough when he engraved some plates for ten shilling notes. He came out about a year ago, and we've had no record of him since. Aged twenty-nine, single, used to have a small flat in Soho, no close relations, educated at Compton. What's he been up to? Forging someone's signature on a cheque?"

"Throwing stones at me," answered Rollison. "Could you dig deeper, find out who he worked for, where he sold his work, friends and associates and that kind of thing, and try to find out if he's been living in England or abroad since he came out of chokey?"

"I will," promised Grice, "on one condition."

"I will tell you everything, in due course," promised Rollison earnestly. "Was he in the forgery racket by himself?"

"We caught him and the printers, but always knew that we missed the main distributors of the forged notes," Grice said. "He might be back at the same game."

"Could be," agreed Rollison.

"How did you come across him?"

"He had the peculiar idea that I was poking my nose into affairs which didn't concern me," said Rollison. "You know how ridiculous that idea was. Bill—"

"I don't know that I like the way you said that," put in

Grice firmly. "Don't take advantage of the fact that the English Channel's between us."

"I don't know much about the job yet," Rollison assured him, "but I've been consulted by a lady in distress. As a result I had my wallet pinched by a man who says he didn't. A Sûreté Nationale official is coming to see me in five minutes' time. If they call you, tell them what an honest, law-abiding citizen I am, will you?"

"If you've been fooling with the French police, God help you," said Grice. "I've always warned you—"

"Just give me a good reference," pleaded Rollison. "I hope to be over to see you tomorrow. Goodbye for now."

He rang off.

Mrs. Dangerfield was waiting in the foyer, pretending to study herself in a mirror in a beautifully carved frame. A small, dapper man in a well-cut suit, and carrying a French style trilby, was standing near the desk. Rollison recognised him at once as Inspector Corbin, of the Sûreté Nationale, an old acquaintance if not quite an old friend. It was too late to tell Mrs. Dangerfield not to take any notice of him, but instead of speaking to her Rollison glanced at her as any man might at a lovely woman, and went straight to Corbin.

Would she take the hint?

"Well, my friend Rollison," said Corbin, in excellent English. "When your name was mentioned it was considered best to allow me to discuss the matter with you." He held out his hand in the casual continental way. "The man you have accused is very angry indeed. Where can we discuss this matter?"

"Let's go up to my room," said Rollison, and turned—and found that Mrs. Dangerfield had not only taken the hint, she had left the foyer.

6

HINT

UNDERNEATH the bed was Simon Roy Shawn.

Sitting near the bed was Inspector Corbin, a man of middle-age, dark-haired, dark-jowled, with thin lips which quirked in a smile, and clear pale grey eyes which missed very little; he has been renowned as a tennis player in his youth, and had the look of litheness and quickness of body and of mind.

He listened . . .

"The question which is of greatest importance, Mr. Rollison, is whether you are in fact telling the truth," he commented with his head a little on one side. "If this man has in fact committed no crime, if you placed the wallet into his pocket—" he paused and shrugged, and undoubtedly he hoped to trick some kind of admission from Rollison.

"Did *what*?" demanded Rollison.

"If the man is telling the truth, then there is only one possibility," said Corbin flatly. "I have discussed this matter at some length with the *agent de police* who was present at the time, and also with two spectators—eye-witnesses, forgive me—and it is evident that you and Benoit had an encounter in the Rue de Rivoli. You went one way, he went the same way."

"The old dodge-and-apologise-while-you-dip-technique," said Rollison.

"What did you say, m'sieu?"

"Sorry," said Rollison. "You must visit London again, and pick up more of the vernacular. Do you seriously believe that I would frame a man like that?"

"If it were to your advantage, yes."

"M. Corbin," said Rollison, mildly, "supposing by some freak of chance I had framed him, can you imagine that I would admit it?"

"No," admitted Corbin with dry amusement. "But it might be interesting to find out what you would say if we were to hold you at the Sûreté for questioning. For, say, two or three days."

"Wouldn't it?" said Rollison, and smiled. "This man Benoit—"

"Yes?"

"Has he a record?"

After a moment's hesitation, Corbin said: "Yes."

"For what?"

"Not for theft and not for picking pockets."

"There's no telling what a man will do if he is desperate," Rollison said. "M. Corbin."

"M'sieu Rollison."

"Could M. Benoit be an artist?"

For the first time, Corbin looked taken aback, and there was no need for him to answer. He shook his head in bewilderment, shrugged again, and took a fold of paper from his inside coat pocket. He unfolded this, and handed it to Rollison. Rollison read a brief account of the statement he had made to the gendarme; after he had read it he took out a fountain pen, signed briskly, and handed it back.

"You understand that you will have to come in person at the first hearing, to swear to this on oath?"

"Yes," said Rollison.

"And it is not your intention to leave the country immediately?"

"I can always come back," Rollison pointed out.

"It would be better if you were to remain in Paris," said Corbin; he stood up. "There is one other thing which you would be well advised to consider, my friend."

"What thing?"

"Benoit is a black-and-white artist, although not very good except in his particular sphere, of engraving," said Corbin. "He is much better than most at that. He earns a reasonable living, even in France in these days of inflation —say, perhaps, an income of two thousand pounds a year. It is enough. There is no reason why he should steal your wallet. Also, he has sufficient money to secure very good legal help. You have doubtless heard of M. Anton Arbier."

"Ah," said Rollison. "Yes. Didn't he handle the defence of old Gustav Prien?"

"Brilliantly."

"Is he acting for Benoit?"

"He is," said Corbin. "And he will insist that you are present in court when the case is first heard. He will enjoy questioning you in front of M. le Prefet. I am telling you, M. Rollison, that it is not always comfortable to be questioned by M. Anton Arbier."

"It will be even less comfortable for M. Arbier when he realises that he is defending a man who specialises in cheating tourists by exchanging bad money for good," Rollison said.

"Are you sure of that?"

"Let me tell you why I'm sure," said Rollison, and told the story of Alice Day.

"We shall investigate closely," Corbin promised. "And the hearing may be tomorrow afternoon or else the morning of the following day, Friday. I would like your assurance that you will not go to England between now and that time."

After a pause, Rollison said: "All right. You have it."

"Very good!" exclaimed Corbin, and turned towards the door.

As he moved, Rollison saw the door of the wide, polished walnut wardrobe move a fraction of an inch. He glanced away as Corbin moved towards the ante-room, apparently satisfied that Rollison would be as good as his word. Rollison let him go ahead, stepped swiftly to one side, and closed the wardrobe doors with a snap; then he turned the key in the lock. He rejoined Corbin, who was already at the passage door with a hand held out.

"I shall enjoy the encounter between you and M. Arbier," he declared. "It will truly be a great occasion!" He shook hands limply, bowed, and as Rollison opened the door, strode out. Rollison left the door ajar and walked with him to the lift, where an elderly man had replaced Albert. The doors closed on Corbin, and Rollison went back to his room. He closed and bolted the door, and went into the bedroom, whistling the air "I'm getting married in the morning". Then he bent down, pushed the bedspread up, and pulled at the bound and gagged body of Simon Roy Shawn. He heard a sharp banging on the wardrobe door, and grinned. A little cloud of dust made him cough, and he wondered how Shawn would feel after the two-hours period of imprisonment. When he discovered that his captor would be able to tell him a great deal about himself, his resistance would probably crumple.

"*Let me out!*" a cry came as if from a long way off.

Rollison hesitated, pulled Shawn free, saw that his eyes were closed; it looked as if he were feigning unconsciousness.

"*Mr. Rollison, let me out!*" came another cry.

Rollison stood up, unlocked the wardrobe door and stood aside. Mrs. Dangerfield almost fell out. Her face was beetroot red, her eyes looked glassy, her lips were set tightly. She went forward, kicked against Shawn, and pitched towards the bed; there was nothing Rollison could do to save her, but she had sufficient presence of mind to turn so that she fell on her shoulder. As Rollison helped her up she glared at him.

"After all, you did go in of your own accord," murmured Rollison.

"It was quite insufferable that you should lock me in!"

"But you might have been a friend of Shawn's," Rollison pointed out. "You might have come for me with a knife or a hammer, and I prefer not to be attacked by thugs who hide in my wardrobe. The first time I was sure that it was you was when you called out."

"You knew who it was perfectly well," said Mrs. Dangerfield, angrily. "I nearly suffocated in there, it was hot enough with the door open a crack. Why on *earth* do you have so many clothes?" She was looking at herself in the mirror, and making magic on her hair with her long fingers; her colour was improving, too. "You made it clear that you didn't want the detective to realise that we were acquainted, but there can be no reason why I shouldn't know what he wanted."

"Well, you know now. There's something else I know too," went on Rollison. "Benoit is an engraver, and he peddles fake currency. Simon Roy Shawn is an engraver who once went to prison for helping to forge treasury notes." He looked down at Shawn, expecting to see his eyes flicker or him to show some sign that he had heard; but there was no movement. "Are you positive—?"

"Did you say Simon *Shawn*?" exclaimed Mrs. Dangerfield.

"Yes."

"But he—why he—but he is one of the clients of my husband's business! Alec thinks he's one of the most promising of the modern artists. He's sold a lot of work for him, keeps trying to find better markets for him. He often talked about Shawn, and says that he doesn't like him as a man, and he's always getting into debt—he's one of those men who can't keep away from the racecourse and the gaming tables. But—"

She broke off, staring down at Shawn.

Rollison looked down, too—and for the first time he stopped thinking that the man was putting on an act. He did not know whether Mrs. Dangerfield knew what had leapt into his mind, whether she felt the same swift surge of horror. He tried not to move too quickly as he went down on one knee beside the man, and felt for his pulse. There was a strange stillness about Shawn's face; there was the same stillness about his pulse; it was not beating. Rollison heard a rustle of movement as Mrs. Dangerfield knelt down beside him, very gracefully; her knees did not touch the floor. She looked over Shawn's body into Rollison's eyes, and there was alarm in hers.

"Is he—dead?"

Rollison didn't speak, but slid his right hand under Shawn's shirt and the singlet beneath it. There was no heart-beat. He looked at the handsome face, saw the slight puffiness at the nostrils, and realised exactly what had happened. Someone had broken into this room and pinched Shawn's nose so that the man could not breathe; a minute of convulsive effort, of terrible struggle for life must have followed. The electric cord held him tight at the wrists and ankles, the adhesive plaster sealed his mouth. Two fingers, or a thumb and forefinger, were all that had been needed to murder this man.

Rollison looked across the body at Mrs. Dangerfield. She caught her breath.

"I didn't do it," she said stiffly. "You can't think I did. I didn't do it."

After a long pause, Rollison asked coldly: "Didn't you?"

7

BODY ON THEIR HANDS

THEY stood up, slowly; it must have looked as if they were operated by the same slack spring. They did not look away from each other for a moment. Rollison reached his full height first but Mrs. Dangerfield only a moment later. Her lips were parted, her hat pushed to one side because of the incarceration in the wardrobe, but Rollison was interested only in those honey-coloured eyes, and the fear in them.

If she had committed this crime, she would have the best possible reason to be frightened. If she had not, she had almost as much to fear.

"Mr. Rollison," she said in a whispering voice, "I tell you that I didn't do it. I can see what happened. Someone held his nostrils tightly, but it wasn't me. I—I hadn't time." She faltered over that, as if realising that the act of murder would not have taken long. The fear seemed to make her eyes black. "You must believe me," she pleaded. "I didn't touch him. I realised that you would bring that detective up here and I had to know what was said, so I came up ahead of you. A maid was just going off duty. She let me in."

"You had plenty of time," Rollison said, "and you had the opportunity."

"I didn't kill him," Mrs. Dangerfield insisted. "If you don't believe me, what chance is there that the police—" She broke off, looked down at Shawn, and closed her eyes.

"Oh, dear God, what is going on?" The question sounded like a prayer. "He was alive when we went downstairs. There isn't any doubt about that. Someone must have broken in while we were having lunch. It was someone else, it wasn't me."

She opened her eyes; they were burning.

"If it was you, you've a lot of other things to answer for," Rollison said.

"Mr. Rollison—" she began, and then broke off as if she realised that she was only wasting words, that he would think whatever the circumstances warranted and she could not influence him. She turned away, went to the dressing-table, and lowered herself to the stool. She sat looking at her own reflection, and at Rollison's. He turned away from Shawn's body, recovered from the shock, but not absolutely convinced that Mrs. Dangerfield was telling the truth.

There had been time for her to kill Shawn, but only just. He had waited two minutes with Corbin in the foyer, they had taken two or three minutes to come up here. So, there had been five minutes, but in that time Mrs. Dangerfield had been anxious and able to hide herself. It wasn't reasonable to think that she had killed this man; she would have been in too much of a hurry to open the wardrobe, push the clothes to one side, get in, and try to make sure that the door didn't swing wide open. She had had to make sure of being able to breathe, and of having a chance to hear everything that was said, too.

She was looking up at Rollison's face, in the mirror.

"If they would kill this man, they will kill others," she said in a taut voice. "Mr. Rollison, I *must* find out whether Alec is alive or dead. I can't help what happens afterwards, I can't help what happens to me, but—find out about Alec. I beg you to. Expense doesn't matter, nothing matters except finding out whether I can do anything to help him."

The plea seemed to come from the heart.

"All right," Rollison said. "I'll find your Alec. After this, I've got to." He paused, and then asked unexpectedly: "What is your first name?"

"Katherine," she answered.

"Katherine Dangerfield," said Rollison, "we have a lot of problems, and at the moment the biggest is a body on our hands. If we tell the police about it, we're bound to be held for questioning. You and I know that we didn't kill Shawn, but the police don't. I doubt if a doctor could estimate the time of death within two hours. So far as the authorities are concerned, he might have been killed before we left the apartment for lunch."

"And I actually *enjoyed* lunch," Katherine Dangerfield said chokingly.

"So if we send for the police and tell the simple truth we'll be held on suspicion," Rollison reasoned, "and that might last for several days. I can pull some strings but not enough to influence the handling of a charge of murder. There's no excuse at all for having bound and gagged Shawn, either, that was taking the law into my own hands. So—"

"We've got to get rid of the body," Katherine Dangerfield said.

Rollison's lips began to pucker.

"Just like that?"

"Of course, if it's possible," she said flatly. Rollison's assurance seemed to have helped her to recover from the shock, and outwardly she was herself again, cool and poised. "Mr. Rollison, I think—"

"As a fellow suspect, I am Richard or Rolly."

"Mr. Rollison, when I told you that I don't mind what

happens afterwards, I meant exactly that. I must find out what has happened to Alec, and I will do anything necessary to give you the opportunity to find him. If—if necessary, I'll say afterwards that you couldn't possibly have killed this man."

"You might not be believed," said Rollison drily. He brushed his hand over his forehead; it was wet with the sweat of anxiety. "I wonder if anyone except his friends the murderers know that he was up here."

"I shouldn't think so," said Katherine Dangerfield.

"You're probably right," said Rollison, but he wasn't thinking about what he was saying, only about the urgent problem of finding somewhere to hide this body. He had told Grice about Shawn, and once Shawn's body was discovered Grice would be after him.

This job wasn't going at all well. On the spur of the moment it had seemed a bright idea to plant that wallet on the little man who had been following Mrs. Dangerfield, and so get him out of the way. At the time Rollison had reasoned quickly that if the man were a rogue the false charge would be a form of rough justice, and if he weren't, it would have to be withdrawn. The last thing he had anticipated was a clash with a man of the eminence of Anton Arbier.

Was that inevitable?

Would a barrister of such calibre and reputation take a brief for a comparatively poor defendant? Surely this meant that Benoit had a lot of money, or wealthy friends. How deep did this affair go? How extensive was the forgery?

"I can see that you're thinking about a dozen things at once, but what are we going to do?" demanded Katherine. "We can't keep him here much longer."

"We can keep him for a while," Rollison said. "We

don't want to dump the body where the police can pick it up quickly."

"Provided it's far enough away from here I don't see that it matters," Katherine said. "We've just got—" Quite suddenly, she put her hand to her forehead and dropped on to the side of the bed. She lost all her colour, even her lips looked pale; Rollison thought that she was going to faint. He moved quickly, put his arms around her, hoisted her towards the head of the bed and lifted her legs up, then tucked pillows behind her shoulders. He found the hooks and eyes and the head of the zipper of her skirt, unfastened it, then unzipped her girdle, which was fastened at one side. She seemed to be oblivious of all this. He went to the cabinet for whisky, poured out a finger, and brought it to her.

And all the time the body of Shawn lay close to the bed on the other side.

Katherine hadn't fainted; she opened her eyes, then moistened her lips as if to make sure she had got all the whisky.

"I—I'll be all right," she said weakly. "That was silly of me. I'll be all right." She closed her eyes, and her lack of colour was alarming; her cheeks seemed made of wax. "Just give me five minutes," she paused, and then went on in a voice which it was difficult to hear: "I've been under a strain such a long time."

Rollison stood back, studying her.

This collapse had been brought on by the shock of finding Shawn dead, of course, but it was not the underlying cause. Probably she had not slept well since her Alec had disappeared and there had been the constant anxiety of the awful question—was he alive or was he dead? All her surface composure, all her quick-wittedness, all her homely matter-of-factness, would serve no purpose until she knew the truth about her husband. And naturally she feared the worst now that she had come face to face with murder. So:

Alec Dangerfield had to be found.

The murderer of Simon Roy Shawn had to be found.

The body had to be hidden . . .

Had it?

Once the police knew about it, he could add a lot of colour to the reason for his trick on Benoit. He could show the smashed stone on the balcony. He could tell the story he had been told by Katherine Dangerfield. If he told Corbin the whole truth, it might save a great deal of trouble and anxiety. At least he would not be on the run, and would not have to waste time getting the body away, for instance, so worsening the situation if it should be traced to him. All he needed was freedom to work on the case. Grice was right; it was much more difficult to work on his own in Paris than in London.

But would the French police allow him any freedom at all once he had told the story? It would have to be the whole truth, or nothing; Corbin would be quick to scent half-truths.

Making a full statement would be taking a big risk, but if it came off he would have a clear run. He could stand up to the questioning, could even stand up to being held on a charge for a few days. That possibility had to be faced, for if things went wrong there was no doubt that he would be held in a Paris prison.

Could Katherine stand that kind of ordeal?

Her eyes were still closed, and she had very little colour, but the waxen pallor of her cheeks had almost gone. She was the most practical and matter-of-fact person he had met for a long time, and quite likely she would listen to reason.

He went to the other side of the bed, pushed the body underneath, stepped to the telephone and ordered tea for two. Then he put in a call to his man Jolly, at his London flat. Jolly had been away for a few days, that was why Katherine had got no answer, but there would be an answer now. Katherine heard him, and turned her head, but she said nothing. Rollison had the impression that all the vitality had been drained out of her.

The tea arrived. Katherine stirred herself to drink it very hot and sweet, and colour began to creep back into her cheeks. Then the London call came through, and she watched as Rollison picked up the receiver, and said:

"Is that you, Jolly? . . . Good man . . . Yes, so Grice tells me, nothing but rain . . . Yes, I am a little involved and there are complications. Jolly, listen very carefully. I want you to catch the next plane to Paris, there's the one at six o'clock which reaches Le Bourget at seven fifteen. I'll be at the airport with Mrs. Alec Dangerfield. I want you to take her back with you to England, and make quite sure that she's safe . . . Yes, I think there might be considerable danger, and the best place will be at the Marigold Club. It's a pity that Lady Gloria has gone on holiday, but Miss Stephenson is a very good stand-in . . . Yes, arrange with Ebbutt to have the club well guarded. We won't tell the police about this, Mrs. Dangerfield's name hasn't been mentioned yet and needn't be. I'll give you more detailed instructions when you reach Le Bourget. There's a plane back to London at nine thirty, and you can catch that . . . Yes, you fix all the tickets. Thanks, Jolly."

He rang off.

Katherine's eyelids were no longer drooping, and her eyes were no longer lack-lustre. Rollison could tell that she wanted to cry: "*Nothing will make me go back to London!*" but instead she said:

"And do you expect me to do just as I'm told?"

"I expect you to realise that you'll only be in the way if you stay here," Rollison answered. "You need a few days absolute rest. I'll do everything I can to find your husband or find out what's happened to him, but if I have to spend part of the time looking after you, I won't have much of a chance."

"I suppose that's reasonable," she conceded, and then unexpectedly she leaned forward, touched his hand, and said: "You're quite right, I will only be a drag on you. I've known for sometime that I would crack up sooner or later. Honestly I don't know how I've kept going as long as I have. Will you—will you tell the police?"

"Some of the story."

"I've been lying here thinking that the damage is done, now, that you're probably quite right, and it's better to come out into the open with it. I couldn't go on for ever keeping everything to myself, with no one to help me. This man who keeps telephoning must know that you're helping me now, and he'll surely know that there's nothing much I can do with you in charge. Will you promise me one thing?"

"If I can."

"Keep me informed all the time."

"Of all major developments, yes."

"Thank you," she said, as if she were fully satisfied, and then she inquired: "Who is this man Ebbutt?"

"An old friend of mine who runs a boxing club and a gymnasium in the East End of London," Rollison told her, "and whenever I need help he always jumps to it. The important thing is to make sure that I needn't worry about you. More tea?"

"No, thank you," Katherine Dangerfield said.

. . . . .

At seven seventeen, the aircraft landed. At seven twenty-seven, he was shaking hands with Jolly, while Katherine studied the elderly, medium sized man with doleful brown eyes, an expression almost of the chronic dyspeptic, the deeply lined sagging skin under the chin, as if he had once been fat and had dieted to the point of folly. There was nothing impressive about Jolly's appearance except his immaculate black coat, a grey cravat with a pearl tie pin, striped trousers and, of course, his bowler hat. He looked as if he belonged to a book of caricatures on *The English At Home.* When he spoke, his quiet pleasant voice gave the impression of complete command and authority. He took charge, it seemed, not only of Katherine but of the Toff.

"Are there any further instructions, sir? I have been in touch with Mr. Ebbutt and with Miss Stephenson, and everything has been arranged as you desired, sir. We will be met at the airport by three of Mr. Ebbutt's men, and shall make quite sure that Mrs. Dangerfield is not followed. If anyone makes an attempt to follow her, he will be followed in turn. In view of the circumstances I felt quite sure that this was a matter in which every risk should be kept to the irreducible minimum."

"And rightly," Rollison said warmly.

"Now I really believe I did the right thing," said Katherine in a clear voice.

"*Are* there any further instructions, sir?" repeated Jolly.

"Yes. Use Ebbutt wherever possible, and find out all you can about Mr. Dangerfield's secretary. What was her name?"

"Betty Oliver," said Katherine.

"Thanks. And also find out all you can about the clients of the art agency. You—"

"I will do everything I can," promised Jolly.

"And find out if any of the men concerned is a good mimic—we're looking for someone who might know Mr. Dangerfield well, and could imitate his voice."

"I'll see to it, sir."

Rollison glanced at Katherine, and she actually laughed; but when she shook hands with him, and said goodbye, she looked pale and tired, and there was nothing like so much vitality in her walk. In the past few hours she seemed to have aged several years. It was almost certainly shock, but could possibly be because of something which Rollison did not yet know about.

He waited until the plane was airborne, then went to telephone Corbin, first at his office, then at his home.

"Yes, certainly," Corbin said. "I will meet you at your hotel room, M. Rollison."

Rollison took a taxi back to the heart of Paris, trying to decide the best way to tell his story, wondering whether its presentation would make the slightest difference to Corbin's reaction. Corbin would have to take it to his superiors, and he would then do what he was told. The facts had to speak for themselves. Rollison sat back in a corner of the taxi, one of the new Citroens which had a scarifying burst of speed, and closed his eyes. It was a strange feeling to think that he might spend the night in a prison cell.

Suddenly, he felt the taxi swing round a corner. The speed did not trouble him, nor the squeal of tyres, but the timing did. He opened his eyes. There was no wide stretch of road ahead, no bright lights, no darting traffic, only the gloom of a side street; they were at least two miles from the Place de L'Etoile. This was no short cut—he knew Paris well enough to be sure of that. He narrowed his eyes. He saw the driver glance round and then pull into the kerb at the corner of a narrower, darker street.

As the taxi stopped, two men moved forward from the shadows.

8

THREE TO ONE

ROLLISON still sat as if he were puzzled by the sudden stop, but he showed no sign of alarm. The taxi driver muttered deep in his throat. One of the men from the shadows moved towards the nearside door, the other towards the door on the left. Rollison moved both arms at the same time, touching the inside handles and pressing them down before either of the men reached the car. The *click-click* as they locked startled the driver, who turned his head in alarm. Rollison, now squatting close to the back of the driver's seat, simply jerked his head and butted the man in the nose. The man squealed and reeled away, tears streaming down his cheeks. The men outside were tugging at the doors. Rollison leaned over and slammed the door next to the driver, then scrambled over the seats. As he dropped into position, the driving door was pulled open again; both men were there.

If they had guns he wouldn't have a chance.

Rollison sat by the blinded driver whose hands were at his face, and who was making little moaning sounds. He heaved his whole body against the man's as if making a a shoulder charge on a football field with a lenient referee. The driver slid along the seat, closer to the men outside. Rollison bumped into him again until he was half in and half out of the taxi. Rollison heard the ticking of the engine, pushed the car into gear and groped for the handbrake; he couldn't see it and wasn't sure where it was.

68

The two men were dragging the taxi driver from his seat so as to get at Rollison, as he touched the handbrake and felt it slacken. The taxi driver was hauled out. One of the other men leaned inside and struck at Rollison with a length of rubber tubing. Rollison bent his elbow and cracked it into the man's face as the car jolted forward.

He thought the engine would stall as he shifted his position so as to be in complete control, the car still going forward in low gear. A man was clutching the open door. Rollison thrust his foot down, and the car roared and lurched forward, the door creaking and cracking. He swung the wheel violently. The man vanished from the door, which swung backwards, and metal cracked and broke. Air streamed in as Rollison reached the nearest street corner, and swung round it. Ahead lay the big main street and the welcome bright lights. He thought he heard running footsteps, but no one loomed up in the driving mirror. The door was still banging against the side of the car, one hinge broken.

Rollison reached the main street, turned left towards the heart of the city and stopped, got out, and pushed the door; it groaned and protested but swung into its proper position, and then he slammed it, the lock held. He got back into the car from the other side, looking towards the corner all the time, but no one appeared to threaten the slightest danger. He drove at a modest forty kilometres an hour, pushing his hair back with his right hand, keeping well to one side so that other cars could pass him. By the time he reached the crazy cacophony which careered round the Arc de Triomphe he was feeling more himself, and drove without difficulty to the George V Hotel. There was ample space outside it, kept clear for patrons by the zealous commissionaires. The one on duty came forward to·open the taxi door, recognised Rollison, and gaped.

"My holiday job," said Rollison lightly. "Let it stay here, will you?" He realised that the man was staring at him as much as at the car, but took no notice of that until he was in the foyer. There two young women, coming from the powder room, looked at him as if appalled. One exclaimed:

"*Mon dieu!*"

He caught a glimpse of himself in a mirror near the lifts. There was a scratch over his right eye which had bled freely, and another on his right temple making him look bloody and battered, all due to the taxi fracas. The lift arrived and the doors opened and a couple came out, obviously Americans. The woman exclaimed:

"For landsakes!"

"Say, are you hurt?" the man asked, while Albert, back on duty, stared up into Rollison's face in alarm.

"Slight accident," said Rollison. "Sorry." He smiled and went into the lift, and Albert hurried after him, pressed the button with exceptional celerity, and shot him upwards. As the lift stopped, Rollison asked: "Has anyone come to see me, Albert?"

"No, sir, no ones."

"Thanks," said Rollison, as the doors opened. "If anyone comes, ask the desk to keep him waiting for ten minutes, so that I can—"

"*Clean up, m'sieu?*" inquired Corbin.

He was by the lift, smiling his droll smile. Albert gaped in surprise. Rollison stepped into the passage and raised his hands in a Gallic fashion which could not be imitated, and turned towards his room.

"Never mind, Albert," Rollison said. "My friends are omniscient." He reached his door and inserted the key, turned it and waited for Corbin to draw level. "You wouldn't care to go in ahead of me, would you?"

"So you expect troubles?"

"They seldom come singly," said Rollison.

Corbin took the handle of the door and thrust it open. He strode through as much as to prove that he was a man of courage.

Nothing happened; there was a slight breeze which made a door rattle, that was all. Rollison followed Corbin, then went into the bathroom. Corbin watched as he bathed the cuts and washed his face; neither of the injuries were serious, and only one was worth a piece of sticking plaster. Rollison brushed back his hair, studied Corbin in the mirror, and tried to guess what attitude the detective would take to the coming story.

"First, how were you hurt?" Corbin asked.

Rollison told him.

"And the taxi, it is still outside?"

"Yes."

"One moment, please," said Corbin and stepped to the telephone. Rollison went to the other side of the bed. The bad moment would come when he actually revealed Shawn's body. At this last minute he wondered uneasily about the wisdom of his decision; would it be wiser to try to hide the body now that Katherine Dangerfield was out of the way? He heard Corbin give instructions for men to come and examine the taxi and to try to find the driver. For the first time there was a reasonable possibility that the authorities would trace one of the men responsible for the series of crimes—but he, the Toff, hadn't a hope.

Corbin finished on the telephone. "So," he said. "What is so urgent that you wish to talk to me privately? I should warn you, Mr. Rollison, I am first a policeman, second a policeman, and third a detective. I might have much sympathy for you, but I have my duty."

"I know all about policemen and their duty," said Rollison. "Before I've finished I shall probably need Arbier's help to get me out of the Bastille. Believe it or not, I planned to come to Paris for a few days holiday, a show or two, and most of all for some food. Did you know that French food is still the best in the world?"

"I have been so informed," said Corbin, gratified even by such blatant flattery.

"And then came complications . . ." began Rollison.

The great difficulty was to explain what had happened without naming Katherine Dangerfield or the fact that Alec Dangerfield was missing. There was a possibility that Corbin had had him followed to the airport and knew about the woman; it was also possible that Corbin had had the telephone to the hotel room tapped, so he might know all about Jolly's instructions and Jolly's task, although Rollison did not think it likely.

He told the story simply, without naming the Dangerfields but saying that the woman had told him that her husband was missing. He related the tale of her following him from the Café de Paris to the Louvre, and had Corbin smiling much of the time; but he felt quite sure that Corbin was expecting a final revelation, and all the time there was this uncertainty about what would happen when the body was revealed.

He showed Corbin the tape machine with the missing wire. He took him on to the balcony, and showed him the broken masonry and the litter of pieces, including several bent rails. He told him of his chase, of bringing Shawn here, of telephoning Grice, of binding and gagging Shawn.

He stopped.

Corbin gave his broadest smile yet.

"And now, you are going to tell me that this man Shawn has disappeared, and you wish me to find him for you," he said. "I am not surprised, perhaps I should say that I am not very much surprised, M. Rollison, but in a way it is remarkable that you have come to me so early. I understand from my friend Superintendent Grice that usually you much prefer to act on your own until you are compelled not to. But—our Paris prisons frighten you, perhaps? Or our French legal customs—that a man is guilty until he is proved innocent. Have you ever paused to think how true that is, M. Rollison? Ask Superintendent Grice, for instance, how often the police arrest a man who *is* innocent. Our way is much the safer way. This lady who has appealed for your help—you have not told me her name."

"No," said Rollison.

"So, you do not intend to." Corbin shrugged. "How different fact is from popular belief. It is the French who are supposed to be gallant, yet here is the Englishman saving the lady's good name by taking great risks himself. First you put a wallet into an innocent man's pocket and accuse him of theft. Second, you sign a statement saying that this is true when you know it is a lie, so you toy with justice. Next, you tie up a man, which was proper enough being in self-defence, it was even praiseworthy, M'sieu— then you assault him when he is defenceless, you go through his pockets, and gag him. What an imposing list of complaints it would be possible to file against you. This name, Shawn—you are sure of it?"

"Yes."

"And he is an artist?"

"Grice told me so."

"And a man from Scotland Yard would never lie," said Corbin drily. "So—do I understand you when I think that you wish me to question Benoit so as to find out whether he has some knowledge of this man Shawn, and where he might be found?"

"You don't understand me," Rollison said. "I brought you here to show you—"

He bent down, and pulled up the bedspread, flinging it over on to the bed, now very uneasy indeed. Even at this late hour he wondered whether he would be wise to get away without telling the truth; it would be quite easy to, Corbin wouldn't expect such a move. Rollison could not bring himself to say that Shawn was dead, and he wanted to study Corbin's expression when he saw the man and realised what had happened.

He bent down as if to tighten his shoelace, and looked under the bed.

Simon Roy Shawn was not there.

"You are not going to produce the rabbit out of the hat, I hope," said Corbin.

"No," said Rollison stiffly. "No." He straightened up slowly, his heart pounding. "He's gone all right. Quite without a trace. And within an hour or two of leaving him, I was attacked on the way from the airport." He moved to the cabinet, and opened it; he had seldom needed a drink so much.

9

CHANCE TO ATTACK

"No," said Corbin, with a polite gesture, "I do not enjoy whisky even if it is Scotch. Thank you, I am quite happy for you to drink alone." He watched Rollison sip, and went on gravely: "I think I understand you, m'sieu. You are aware that an encounter with M. Arbier would go badly for you in the court, you are sure that this man Benoit has an association with your attackers, and the assailants of this mysterious woman." He smiled. "You do not wish to face Arbier in court knowing that he would almost certainly compel you to tell the truth—but of course, before letting it go so far you would tell the truth, and the charge would be withdrawn. Ah. Now I *fully* understand."

His eyes were very bright.

"I thought you would," said Rollison warily.

"You wish to have Benoit held on this charge for a few days, so that you will have your opportunity to investigate further—and the only way you can do that is to make the clean breast of everything. So, you hope that I am an understanding man. M. Rollison, I have a piece of very good news for you."

Rollison's heart leapt.

"In the course of investigations into the activities of the man Benoit, it has been discovered that he had a number of forged British, French and German currency notes in his possession," Corbin beamed. "And more were discovered at his house. As you told me, it is obvious that he is an agent for a gang of forgers—much forged money has been distributed in Paris in recent weeks—and but for your charge against him they would not have been found, so there is much goodwill towards you at the Sûreté. For the time being, you understand, it would be unwise to overplay your luck! At all events, M. Rollison, the lesser charge of the theft of the wallet is now unimportant. The major charge of being in possession of forged currency, that is very different indeed. So, it will take some time to prepare the case. M. Arbier, on being advised of this, agrees that it would not be wise for him to insist on the hearing of the first charge. It is, so to speak, suspended. If Benoit should be found guilty of issuing these notes, then the sentence would be much more severe than one for picking pockets. Does all this make you feel happier?"

"Much," said Rollison, and he thought of Alice Day and her hopeful Mike, as well as many others who suffered this miserable kind of fraud.

"I am very glad also," said Corbin. "As for this man Shawn—yes, it is possible that Benoit will be able to tell us where to find him. By the time I return to my office, I am hoping that the taxi driver will have been found and questioned, also. I think you can sleep easily tonight, m'sieu."

"I know I shall," said Rollison.

"Are you sure you would not like me to know the name of the lady? It is possible for me to examine the passenger list of the aircraft, and you will cause only a short delay."

"A man of honour," said Rollison solemnly, "cannot betray a trust."

Corbin's eyes lit up.

"Surely M. Rollison, you are the most old-fashioned man of my acquaintance! But to meet a man whose word is his bond—it is most refreshing. I enjoy it. However, I have one thing to ask of you."

"Yes?" said Rollison cautiously.

"I must ask that from now on you will make no attempt to find this man Shawn. You will not look for him."

Rollison said, slowly: "That's a pity."

"I do not understand what—oh, I see. A *peety*. You mean that you will not give me that assurance?"

"No."

"So," said Corbin, frowning, but there was still a bright light in his eyes. "Yes, it is a peety. I shall have to report this matter to my superiors, and they may decide that some restriction must be placed upon your movements. On the other hand they may take a different view, and I shall not need to report immediately. Certainly not until tomorrow morning, M. Rollison. I think I shall ask you again tomorrow."

"M. Corbin," said Rollison warmly, "you are a man after my own heart."

.   .   .   .   .

One thing was certain now, Rollison reasoned when Corbin had gone; he would have to swear that he had last seen Shawn alive, and so would Katherine. He did not think there would be much trouble, provided he could tell Katherine what she must say before the police asked questions. If Shawn were found tonight, Corbin would telephone the Yard, the Yard would go to Jolly, and Grice would probably check whether any new guests were at the Marigold Club—that club for lonely ladies owned and operated at a loss by his Aunt Gloria. It was particularly fitting that even in her absence, Lady Gloria should be helping; after all, she had sent Alice to him in such trouble.

Alice was lucky to be out of it.

Rollison had the night to work and to think in. It was nearly nine o'clock, and among other things he was hungry, but he was in no mood to be fussed over by Pierre or the other waiters downstairs. He telephoned for a steak and *pommes frites*, finished his whisky, and lay on his back on the bed—just where Katherine Dangerfield had been. So much had happened that it would be easy to lose sight of the main quest: for Alec Dangerfield, dead or alive.

Dangerfield, running an art agency; and one of his protégés a forger.

Dangerfield was a man of independent means, if his wife were right, and there was no reason why she shouldn't be. Was it possible that Dangerfield's considerable income really came from the proceeds of forgery?

"I'm beginning at the wrong end," Rollison argued. "It's no use guessing about Dangerfield. Jolly might get something from or on this Betty Oliver or the Art Agency, I want an angle in Paris." He leaned back, hands locked behind his head, and gave himself over to concentrated thought. "Shawn was here and under the bed. I was out for some hours. Someone had to get in, carrying the body which would be stiff with *rigor* by then, and get it down those narrow stairs."

He paused.

"Would they?" he asked himself softly. "Would they?" He got up, and went to the balcony. A cool wind blew off the Seine, and, down below, the lights of the cars moving along the Champs Elysées, of the shops and restaurants, of the cinemas and showrooms on either side of the street suggested a hot frenzy of motion. The French windows of the apartment next to his were tightly closed, and the shutters were half down. Rollison remembered that fat woman sitting at her dressing-table, screaming. He remembered how she had stared at him. And he remembered that she had failed to identify him when she had come with the house detective and the Assistant Manager's Assistant. He studied the adjacent balconies. It would be comparatively easy to hoist a corpse from one to the other, on a board, or a kind of homemade stretcher. He went back into the room and telephoned the Assistant Manager, whose Assistant was still on duty.

"I've been wondering whether you caught the thief," Rollison said, brightly. "It isn't nice to think that one might be wandering about the hotel."

"It is not, sir," said the Assistant Manager's assistant in perfect English. "In point of fact, no one was apprehended, but there has been no report of theft, and I have every reason to believe that it was a false alarm."

"Really?" Rollison sounded intrigued.

"Yes, sir. The incident was first reported from an office on the other side of the Champs Elysées, and with the house detective I made immediate calls upon the apartments on the top floor, and later every apartment. The lady in the apartment next to yours agreed that she had seen a man, whom she believed to be a workman, and as no workmen were active on the roof at that time, she was good enough to see if she could recognise the man. However, as no one was discovered it was not necessary to trouble her further."

"No, of course not," said Rollison understandingly. "Most public spirited of her. An English lady, I believe."

"No, indeed not, sir, a Frenchwoman. Madame Blanc."

"Ah, Madame Blanc," said Rollison. "I was getting her mixed up with someone else. Thank you very much."

"Your service, Mr. Rollison," the Assistant Manager's Assistant said.

Rollison rang off, smiling more broadly, but almost on

the instant there came a tap at the door. He was wary at first but had no need to be; this was the floor waiter, complete with an entrecôte, pommes *frites*, an oozing Camembert, butter, bread, and a bottle of Chateau Rille, 1955. Rollison ate more heartily than he would have an hour ago, and when the steak was finished, cut a piece of Camembert carefully, spread four creamy dabs on four smaller pieces on a long piece of crusty bread, ate a little, then lifted the telephone and asked for Room 81—the room next to his. There was a long pause before the operator said:

"There is no answer, m'sieu."

"I'll try again later," Rollison said. He finished the cheese with relish and the wine with a sigh, ate several grapes, and then sent for the waiter to take the trolley table away. When he was alone, he telephoned Madame Blanc's room again, and the answer was still the same.

He rang off, took out the many-bladed knife, went to his own door, studied it, and saw that the ordinary skeleton key was the best tool for opening it; whoever had broken in here this morning had probably used one. He closed his own door and went to Madame Blanc's, checked that the lifts were on the ground floor, and slid the skeleton key into the keyhole. It needed only a minute's twisting to get a grip and turn the lock. The indicator at the lifts showed that both were still on the ground floor. He pushed the door open and stepped inside, then closed the door so that he was in darkness—inside an anteroom exactly the same as his, but with the doors and the furniture in the opposite positions. He switched on the light. The furniture was identical with his, so were the wallpapers, the *décor* generally. He put on the light of the bedroom, then put out that in the anteroom, and closed the bedroom door. Everything was the same as in his, even to the colour of

the bedspread. He looked under the bed but found nothing. The bathroom was empty. He found the wardrobe
doors locked, remembered locking Katherine Dangerfield
in, but did not smile. His heart began to thump. He unlocked the door, expecting to find Shawn's body toppling
on to him.

It did not: there were women's clothes, that was all.

He drew back, locked the wardrobe again, and looked
about him, but he was beginning to think that he had been
wrong; or else that Shawn's body had been moved from
here as well as from his own room. Where else could a
body be hidden if—?

He looked up to the top of the wardrobe, and saw a
heavy quilted bedspread at one end. He hauled a chair
close and stood on it.

Shawn was there, half covered by the bedspread.

.   .   .   .   .

There was a deep recess at the top of the wardrobe, undoubtedly there for storing suitcases. The recess had
room for Shawn, whose legs were bent a little, and whose
head was tucked down towards his chest. Rollison ad-
justed the spare blanket which had been thrown over
carelessly to catch the eye if anyone glanced up, then
climbed down again. There could be no doubt now; the
group he was fighting did not want him in danger from
the police—and, obviously, feared what he could tell them.
Shawn hadn't been killed to frame him, Rollison—so
Shawn had been killed to make sure he couldn't give away
vital information.

It was impossible to believe that a normal hotel visitor
had been prevailed upon to help this plot against him.
Rollison knew Madame Blanc must have been planted in
that apartment so as to be next to him; it must have been
pre-arranged. Yet he had not talked to Katherine

Dangerfield until that morning, no one could have been sure that he would become involved. Unless she had been followed to London, or unless her telephone had been tapped when she had talked to Jolly. There was another possibility; that his interest in Benoit had been noticed, and that this was an involved method of finding out the reason for that interest. Certainly Madame Blanc might have been planted in the room next door by friends of Benoit. The important thing now was to find out where Madame Blanc had gone, whom she worked for, who she was. This was an angle that Corbin wasn't likely to get on to for some time and it offered the chance that Rollison needed desperately.

He began to search the room.

He wasn't surprised that there was nothing to help him trace Madame Blanc. There were no letters, no initials or labels on the two suit-cases, nothing that helped him on her clothes although the police might find the makers' names useful.

He worked quickly, methodically and silently, and after fifteen minutes was quite sure that he had overlooked nothing. His chief hope now was to find Madame Blanc herself, and the fact that she had left the luggage and the clothes behind suggested that she was coming back.

Then he heard a sound in the passage. He stepped swiftly to the door, flicked off the light, and stood alongside the wardrobe, close to the wall. A key turned in the lock and light shone through as the door opened.

A man stepped in.

10

NIGHT WORK

ROLLISON pressed back into the corner between the ward-robe and the wall. Unless the man came right into the room he would not be seen. He heard the door close, and immediately the ante-room light shone out. The soft *click* told of stealth; this man was no more anxious to be heard than Rollison had been.

Had he come for the body?

Rollison heard his cautious footsteps, and judged that he was a big man. The room light went on. Rollison nar-rowed his eyes against it, and tensed himself ready for an attack if the other came in sight, but he could not believe that the man suspected that anyone was here.

The footsteps drew nearer.

They stopped. Rollison heard heavy breathing, then a creaking sound, and realised that the stranger was looking at the top of the wardrobe, holding the decorated edge so that he could haul himself up on his toes and make sure that the body was still there. The creaking stopped. A key turned in the wardrobe. The door banged back. Rustling sounds followed, puzzling at first, but suddenly Rollison realised that the man was taking out the clothes. Rollison ventured close to the edge of the wardrobe, and saw the suit-case on the foot of the bed. The man turned round laden, and put the clothes in slowly and neatly—he didn't just dump them. He went to the dressing-table, opened each drawer, took out the few oddments which

Rollison had seen there, and placed these in the case. Had he turned round at that moment he would have seen Rollison, who was poised for the attack.

Each time, the man turned without coming close to the hiding place.

He went into the bathroom; there were sounds as of glass tapping against a plate glass shelf, and a rattling before the man came back. Rollison did not see him this time, but heard the lid of the case fall. There was a pause and the man sighed, as if with relief. A match scraped, and cigarette smoke from an American-type cigarette teased Rollison's nostrils. Rollison saw the end of the blue suit-case as the man lifted it, then heard the footsteps again; a moment later, the room light went out, so did that in the anteroom. The door opened and fainter light shone into the room from the passage.

The door closed.

Rollison said: "Not bad," and wiped the sweat off his forehead as he went forward and plucked up the telephone. "Hallo! Porter, please." He held on, every second age-long, until the porter answered in French. "This is M. Rollison. There is a man coming down the stairs or in the lift carrying a blue suit-case," Rollison said. "Delay him for five minutes, will you, until you see me in the hall."

"Very good," the porter said. "How shall I recognise the gentleman?"

"He's tall, heavily built, and carrying the dark blue case."

"I will delay him, sir. But if he is taking his luggage—"

"If he doesn't pay his bill, I will," said Rollison. "Call a taxi for me and have it wait, and don't let the man leave until I've gone out."

"Very good, sir," the porter said, and the tone of his

voice gave no hint that he thought he was dealing with a lunatic. Rollison went to the door, opened it a crack, and saw the man disappearing into the lift; so he was brazening this out, which was probably the safest way to get out of the hotel. Rollison let him get half-way down before pressing for the other lift, which began to move up at once. When he stepped into the ground floor foyer, a heavily-built man carrying the blue case was talking to the porter; crisp notes were changing hands. Rollison went past without glancing right or left, and turned away from the Champs Elysées towards the narrower darker streets. He stood between two cars, and saw the man from Madame Blanc's apartment step out, case in hand. The commissionaire asked: "*Taxi, m'sieu?*"

"Sure," the man said.

The single, simple word set Rollison's mind racing, for only an American could say 'sure' like that.

Rollison moved near to him as a taxi turned the corner; and almost immediately a second taxi followed. Rollison saw the first one stop; the man's figure blotted out the lights for a moment. Then in that unmistakably American voice he said:

"*Gare du Nord, tout de suite.*"

"*Si, m'sieu.*"

The man clambered in, the taxi jolted off, and the other pulled up just behind it. Rollison was already hurrying.

"Follow that taxi. I think it is going to the Gare du Nord," he said, and got in.

This was exactly the same model Citroen as the cab in which he had travelled from the airport, and he contemplated the back of the youthful driver's neck for a few seconds, then looked at the other taxi.

Would the big American go to the station, or would he change his orders?

For nearly twenty minutes, it looked as if the station was the true destination, but suddenly the taxi turned off the main streets towards the river, reached the right bank, and began to put on speed. So did Rollison's. When they reached the bridge near the Louvre, the lights were in their favour and they swung over it. On the left bank, the taxi ahead took a right turn, into the Rue des Saintes Pères, which Rollison knew well as the best antique shopping district of Paris. A number 87 bus lumbered past; so his prisoner had probably come here to see the same quarry.

It took another turning right.

"Go slowly past that street," Rollison ordered his man, and glanced towards the right, saw the brake lights of the first taxi glowing a very bright red, and knew that this was his lucky night after all. "Stop, please," he said a moment later, and thrust ample payment over the driver's shoulder and was climbing out of the taxi before the man could ejaculate a startled *merci*. Rollison closed the cab door quietly, for all his haste, and stepped to the corner.

The other taxi was moving off. The big man was standing thirty yards or so away, with the suit-case at his feet, looking up and down the street. He lit a cigarette from a pack of *Camels*. Rollison did not show himself, and the man turned, picked up the case, opened a door and disappeared. Rollison saw the door close, judged that it was two removed from a lamp post, and stood where he was while three Lambrettas and two bubble cars hurtled along the street, smelly and noisy. When they had gone there was a moment's uncanny silence; then Rollison turned into the street—the Rue Morot.

He went closer, watching the doorway intently in case the big man came out again; the way he had looked up and down the street suggested that he thought that he might be followed. No one appeared. A cat squawked, a dog barked, a car honked just behind him. He reached the doorway, a small one set in a larger one, which meant that it led to a kind of courtyard, and that there were several apartments beyond. He turned the handle and thrust, and the door opened. It creaked, alarmingly. He stepped through and closed the door as quietly as he could. There was the cobbled yard he had expected, with three doorways leading off it, over each of them a dim electric lamp was burning. On the right was a fourth doorway marked *Concierge* and a brighter light shone in there; an old woman sat nodding, an old man sat reading a newspaper—*Paris-Soir*. Neither of them looked up, and Rollison went to the first doorway. The door was open, there was a narrow flight of stairs, twisting away out of sight— but there was no smell of tobacco smoke. He went to the next doorway. Here the stairs were wider, and the first landing seemed nearer; more important, there was the unmistakable smell of American cigarette tobacco.

Rollison started up the stairs.

It was quiet and eerie. Only a single yellow light burned at the ceiling, a long way up, and down here he could hardly see his own feet. The carpet was threadbare, the frayed edges kept catching his shoes. He reached the first landing, and took out a pencil torch to shine on a white card which read:

M. DUBONNET
MME. DUBONNET

Stairs stretched a long way upwards, as far as he could judge there were three more flights. The smell of cigarette tobacco was still noticeable, and unless the man had come up this far it would have disappeared by now. He did not pause at the next three landings, but reached the top, where another white card was stuck in a small bracket. He switched on his torch, and read:

GABRIEL SMITH
Black and White Artist

Rollison smiled his deep satisfaction, and switched off the torch. This was far too much for coincidence; the big man was almost certainly Gabriel Smith, or else had come here to visit the man. And the woman certainly wouldn't have been registered under her own name at the hotel— he would never have traced her had he not followed the man. There were two ways to handle the situation: to break in now and confront the American, or to wait until it was dark and everyone was asleep before breaking in. All Rollison's inclination was to ring the bell and wait to enjoy the consternation the sight of him was bound to create, but the sensible thing was to search the apartment secretly, before revealing himself. The more he knew, the easier it would be to deal with Smith.

But if he found nothing incriminating, but was caught on enclosed premises and the police were called, it would be far more difficult to explain.

He took out the torch again and studied the lock; like those on so many old houses in Paris, it was old fashioned, and could easily be forced; but these high double doors often had hefty bolts. He pushed one side of the doorway gently; it was not bolted now. He examined it more closely and saw a gap at the top, where it sagged away from the door frame. He could even see that it was bolted. There was a good chance that the bolt did not fit, and even if it did he could work it loose—provided he could find something to stand on.

He had seen an old chair in the courtyard.

He wedged a matchstick into the door, so that he would

know if it had been opened when he came back, and went downstairs, attracting no attention, strolled along the Rue des Saints Pères, went into a little *bistro* and ordered a pernod. There were half a dozen metal tables outside, and some close to the window inside; he chose one of those, for he could see the corner of the Rue Morot and would know if Madame Blanc or Gabriel Smith appeared again to-night.

They did not.

He sat waiting until a little before midnight, every incident and aspect of the affair making a pattern in his mind, and his sense of excitement increased all the time. The connection between Alec Dangerfield, the artist's agent, and the three artists themselves—Benoit, now on a charge, Shawn dead, and Gabriel Smith at home with Madame Blanc's clothes, seemed to point only to one thing: a chain of engravers making plates for large-scale forgery.

One French, one English and one American artist were at work, each a specialist in his own currency forgery. Could the forgery be on such an international scale?

Just after midnight, Rollison paid his bill and was watched by a drowsy looking barman as he went out, strolled first towards the river, and then towards the Rue Morot. Everything was exactly the same as when he had been here before except that fewer lights glowed at the windows and more shutters were closed.

Inside the courtyard of the apartment house where Smith had gone, the dim lights were on, but the concierge's room was in darkness. Rollison took the old chair from the yard and carried it on his shoulder up the stairs, careful not to trip up over the threadbare carpet. The matchstick was still in position. He waited at the top floor for several minutes, listening intently but hearing no sound.

Then he used his picklock, and the lock turned easily. He pushed at the door; it was caught at the top, and would not open. He climbed up on the chair and saw the gap between the two narrow doors and the darkness beyond. His torch shone on the bolt, and using a pair of pincers which looked like blunt scissors, he gripped the bolt and gradually slid it back. He made a little noise, but no other sounds came from outside or inside the apartment.

The doors sagged.

He got down, put the chair aside cautiously, and went into the apartment. Ahead lay a narrow passage, with doors leading to the right and left. He half expected to hear a man snoring, but did not. He turned right, and shone his torch about. A door stood ajar. He pushed this open, and swivelled his torch about a studio with a huge north light. Here was a drawing board, easel, inks and paints, instruments for precision drawing, everything one would expect to find in the studio of a black-and-white artist who had ambitions in colour.

Rollison turned away from this room; before he could start searching in earnest he had to make sure that no one could interrupt him. He took it for granted that Smith and 'Madame Blanc' would be here together, perhaps were man and wife. It might be necessary to tie them up and gag them—as he had Shawn. The thought sobered him, until he reminded himself that one or the other might have killed Shawn.

Was that assuming too much?

Wasn't it more true to say that they knew who had killed the English artist?

Rollison pushed open another door, and on the right saw a pale street light shining into a bedroom. It was utterly silent, and that puzzled him; men of Smith's size and rather chesty breathing usually snored or at least breathed very heavily. Rollison stood listening, intently.

There was certainly no sound of breathing; it wasn't just that whoever was in the room was breathing softly. He pushed the door wider open. There was a big double bed, and the street light shone on the corner of a pillow, and spread a faint glow about the rest of the room. There was Gabriel Smith—or at least, the big man—and there was Madame Blanc. The bed was plenty big enough even for two such bulky people.

Rollison stepped inside the room, approached and stopped abruptly. Then he stood looking down at the couple, feeling sure that they were dead. The stillness, that utter silence, could only mean one thing. He felt an icy chill creeping up his body as he moved the sheet to one side, and took the man's wrist—exactly as he had taken Shawn's earlier that day. There was no movement at all, and there was no movement at the woman's pulse.

Rollison stood back, the icy coldness creeping over his whole body. There was more than the shock of this discovery; there was the overwhelming realisation of the ruthlessness of the murderers.

It did not even occur to him to think that these deaths could be suicide.

11

FIND

ROLLISON went out of the presence of death.

He stood by the half open door, badly shaken, picturing the woman as she had sat at her hotel window, plump, hearty, healthy looking, sensual. He went to the front door, where the long bolt was rusty and difficult to move, but he pushed it into its socket, then switched on the light in the hall which was little more than a narrow passage. He saw light gleaming on white cups and saucers and crockery, stepped into a small kitchen, and switched on that light, too. It overlooked the drab courtyard. He studied the empty coffee cups and wine glasses on the draining board; nothing had been washed up, and dregs of red wine looked like blood. Plates stacked from an evening meal, apparently an omelette and boiled new potatoes. He picked up the coffee cups and sniffed at the dregs, but could not be sure whether any poison was there. The blood red wine moved sluggishly in the bottoms of the glasses. He spent no more time in here, but went to the studio. There was no danger of being seen through the big north light, so it was safe to flick the switch. A clear, bright fluorescent glow shone over some drawing boards, and on to a closed box. Rollison opened the box.

Pinned to the lid were three United States Currency bills—of one, five, and ten dollar values. In the box were the tools of an engraver, the fine cutting implements which could be used with such precision. Near the box were several powerful magnifying glasses. There was little doubt that someone, presumably Gabriel Smith, had engraved the half-finished plates, using the genuine currency to work from. It was easy to imagine the long hours of painstaking care put into each small section of the plate, the enormous value if anyone could produce notes good enough to pass as genuine. And as there was a lot of forged currency about, this suggested that it was a long term process, needing new plates.

Rollison left the box open, and began to search the room. In one corner was a cupboard filled with ink and paint, old rags, empty tubes from which the last touch of paint had been squeezed, brushes which looked as if they had never been cleaned. Against one wall was a large cabinet of the kind in which plans and charts and blue prints were kept, and he opened the top drawer. Inside were sheaves of letters and some books and some files. He began to feel hopeful, but then realised that everything here had been picked over; nothing he read seemed to have any significance, none of the letters bore a recent date. Would this search be a waste of time too? He felt worse because he could so easily have come and talked to Smith and the woman, he might have been able to frighten them into talking; instead, he had let them be killed.

Why had it been necessary to kill them?

It was a waste of time asking himself that question.

He searched every drawer, found innumerable sketches in black-and-white and colour, kept turning them over to see if there was any address on the back, and suddenly found four in a row all stamped:

Dangerfield Art Agency,
Greville Street,
W.C.2.

Quite suddenly, he was filled with a fresh sense of urgency.

Now it was time he went to London, talked to Betty Oliver, looked at Dangerfield's records, and tried to find the key to the mystery there. Unless there was something in Smith's pocket or in the woman's handbag, there was nothing more to help him here. He went back into the bedroom, and put on the light. It was strange to look upon two dead people who seemed to be sleeping. Smith's clothes were on a chair, the jacket neatly draped, the trousers folded. It was obvious that the drug had been put into the wine or the coffee before Smith had come back, for no one had been here since his return; the bolted front door proved that. At least he had the first chance to search the clothes and the handbag.

Smith's wallet was fat and old; dog-eared letters seemed to spill out of it, it probably hadn't been cleared out for years. Even the man's passport was wedged in it. The woman's handbag was different; everything was clean and tidy. There was a little paper money, and a bill from the hotel. Rollison put the handbag aside, and looked at the wallet; it would take half an hour to go through this, for every note in it should be studied. He opened the wallet as a car turned the corner, travelling very fast, and made him raise his head to listen. It scorched along the street, and seemed to stop right outside. He stood up quickly and went towards the window, keeping to one side so that he could see out without being seen. Car doors slammed. He peered out, and saw three men striding away from the car.

One of the men was Corbin.

.   .   .   .   .

Rollison pushed Smith's wallet into his pocket, and stepped towards the front door. It was essential not to be found here, the police must never know he had been. He stretched up for the bolt, debating whether he had time to get downstairs, or whether he ought to break into another flat to hide. Then he heard footsteps—two men were coming up the stairs, and he heard one speak in a low-pitched voice. They made it impossible for him to go out this way.

He swung round.

The kitchen which overlooked the courtyard was probably the safest way out. He pushed close to the window, opened it and peered down. Corbin and one other man were disappearing into the building, and no one appeared to be on guard. If anyone was, it would probably be by the police car. Rollison pushed the window wide open. It had a tiny balcony, little more than an extension of the window ledge with a knee-high rail round it. Other tiny balconies were on either side, but neither was within reach.

A bell rang inside the flat.

Rollinson looked downwards. Balconies identical with this were at the three windows beneath him, and it was a long way down to the cobbles. The bell rang again; soon the men would start making a commotion which might wake the neighbours. Rollison climbed over the balcony, and lowered himself at full length; his feet just touched the railing of the one below. He released his hold on the higher rail gingerly, stood balanced on the one beneath, and bent his knees until he was able to lean against the wall. Very cautiously he stepped down on to the railing of the balcony of the flat below. He heard banging, and others in the apartments were bound to be roused. He had to go down to two more balconies though, and the first had been nerve-racking enough.

At least the cobbles were much nearer.

A light went on in the flat just above his head, and shone out vividly. If he had been by that window a few seconds earlier, he would have been seen. Anyone opening a window and pushing out an arm would make him lose his balance. The banging seemed further away, but another light went on across the courtyard, and from there some-one was almost certain to look out. He had to go through the manoeuvre again, and now his nerves were on edge; he half expected a scream of alarm from the window opposite or the window above.

He heard a distant thudding, and was sure that the police were trying to break down Smith's door.

He reached the bottom window until all he had to do was lower himself to arm's length and drop a foot or two. Edginess faded. He hung suspended for a moment before dropping down, his knees bent to take the strain. A mo-ment later he stood quite still in the courtyard, while people looked from the windows, someone shouted and, as he had feared from the moment he had stepped out, a woman screamed.

He saw her outlined against the nearest window.

He kissed his hand to her, and turned towards the doors leading to the street, pulling up the collar of his coat so as to hide his face. He heard a footstep just outside. The small inner door began to open. He stood behind it until a man's hand appeared; then a foot. Rollison thrust the door back. The man cried out and snatched his hand out of the way, but his foot was trapped. Rollison pulled the door wide, saw the man hopping on one foot, gave him a push and sent him toppling. Then he raced towards the corner.

Corbin might have left another man there.

Rollison swung round into the Rue des Saints Pères, saw two small cars and a motor scooter, as well as several couples walking along arm-in-arm. He turned in the other direction, towards the Seine, running very fast. No one was in his way, but the couples must be gaping. He reached the river bank as the control lights changed, and traffic surged towards him; among it was a taxi with its lighted sign "*Libre*". He shouted at it, and the driver shouted back and drove on. He waited for the stream of traffic to pass, then crossed to the river side. Any moment the police might arrive. Once Corbin realised what had happened he would send out radio calls for assistance, and he would probably send immediately to Rollison's hotel.

If he could only get a taxi . . .

He saw one swinging round from the bridge, darted across the road, hailed it, and it slowed down. Two minutes later he was being driven across the river, and the night traffic was too slight to slow the taxi down.

. . . . .

As Rollison opened the door of his room half an hour later, the telephone bell began to ring. He strode towards it, snatched it up and asked in a faint, tired-sounding voice:

"Who's that?"

"I wish to speak to Mr. Rollison," Corbin said, very crisply.

"Rollison here," Rollison said. "Who is that? I—oh Corbin! Dammit, man, it must be nearly two o'clock."

"It is not yet one o'clock," Corbin said. "I am sorry to disturb you, but I have some questions to ask. Do you know of an American named Smith—Gabriel Smith?"

This was a moment to lie.

"No," answered Rollison flatly.

"Are you sure?"

"Yes."

"Do you know of a woman named Bertine Blanc?"

"No," answered Rollison. He lowered himself to the bed and leaned back on the pillows. He could speak more freely now, because he was breathing less heavily. He had come in through the service entrance and walked up the service stairs, and his heart was still thumping from the exertion. "Do you have to ask me all this in the middle of the night?"

"What time did you get in this evening?"

"I went out for a walk after you'd left," Rollison said, and knew that once Corbin began to check, he would know that these were lies; but it was possible to confide in the police too much, he could place too much reliance on Corbin's willingness to turn a blind eye. "Why, what's happened?" Rollison demanded.

"I will see you later," Corbin said, and rang off abruptly.

He probably felt sure that Rollison had escaped from the apartment on the Rue Morot, and most likely would send a man over to check the story. The night porter who had been on duty when Rollison had left would soon give the game away, and his description of the man with the blue suitcase would be quickly recognisable as Smith. The choice lay between waiting here and trying to brazen it out with Corbin, or leaving Paris and trying to get to England. Corbin might find enough evidence to justify holding him while in Paris, but not enough to send to Scotland Yard. He might get that later but he couldn't have it yet.

"But if he has the airport watched, I've had it," Rollison said. "And he probably has."

He stood quite still, staring at the balcony window, until suddenly he remembered that he had Gabriel Smith's passport in his pocket.

12

"MR. SMITH"

THE passport, flimsier than an English one and with a soft cover, gave Gabriel Smith's height as six feet two; and Rollison was nearly that. It gave his hair as brown, and Rollison's was dark brown. It gave his eyes as grey-blue and Rollison's were grey. It said nothing about any "special peculiarities", and nothing about weight; Smith must be three stone heavier than Rollison. He had been born, the passport announced, in Scranton, New Jersey. Rollison pushed this and Smith's wallet in his inside pocket, his own passport in his hip pocket, put on a raincoat, and went out. He did not know whether Corbin had already sent local police to watch the hotel. Probably he had.

The night porter was busy with two bright young things who had just come back from a *Paris By Night* tour. Rollison slipped past him. No commissionaire was on duty, and most of the parked cars were gone. Rollison walked towards the Champs Elysées, half expecting to see a police car turn the corner. There was some traffic about, but it might be a long time before he was lucky again with a cab, but the important thing was to get away from the hotel. Two gendarmes were strolling along, chatting. A traffic gendarme's whistle shrilled, and an unexpectedly large mass of traffic surged forward. No taxis with lighted signs were among them. He turned round and a man came towards him out of the shadows.

So Corbin—

"You want nice young lady for nice night?" the man asked, softly. "I take you to nice young lady."

"In a car?"

"Yes, sair, in a very good car. I—"

"You want nice fat fee to take me to Le Bourget?"

"Pardon, m'sieu?"

"How much to take me to Le Bourget?"

"With nice lady?"

"By myself."

The man considered. "Twenty dollairs," he announced at last. The light showed his thin features and thin hair and his pallor.

"Five pounds," said Rollison.

"Okay," the man said eagerly.

The "very good" car was an old Citroen which creaked and rattled along. Rollison sat next to the driver and wondered whether the nice lady would be as old as the car or as ready to fall to pieces. He kept looking round, but they weren't followed, so after a while he lit a cigarette and sat back comfortably. The driver began to talk. Rollison let him, answering in grunts and monosyllables, and he remembered Gabriel Smith's tell-tale "*sure*". With an American passport, remember, he had to speak like an American.

.   .   .   .   .

There was a seat on a plane leaving at four-thirty, a KLM. The French officials looked tired, glanced at Rollison casually, stamped Smith's passport, and did not trouble to wish him *bon voyage*. The plane left on time. At a quarter to six it touched down at London airport, and at five to six a Customs official said:

"Hope you have an enjoyable time in England, Mr. Smith."

Rollison looked astonished.

"Why, that's very nice of you," he said. "Very nice indeed." He made the "very" sound more like "vurry" but as he used the words he thought of the man who had taken him to Le Bourget, and wanted to laugh; then he remembered Smith's "Sure", and his strange stillness as he had lain next to the woman.

Rollison strode out, free as the air, into the grey light which promised more rain. It was beginning to fall when he reached Gresham Terrace, where Jolly would be sleeping the sleep of the just. He had been concentrating so hard on what had happened, trying to make sense of it and trying to make sure what he should do next first, that he had paid no attention to the vastness of London, to the narrow crowded streets, to the spaciousness and graciousness of Mayfair.

He paid off the cabby, went to the front door, then looked up and down, hardly able to believe that he had reached home safely and that no one had followed him. He kept assuring himself that no matter what Corbin said to Bill Grice, there was nothing that Grice would or could do in England for the time being.

Gresham Terrace was a short street of tall, grey-roofed, grey-faced houses, most of them newly painted. A fitful gleam of sunshine brightened the film of rain on the pavements and the smooth road. Rollison opened the front door with his key and stepped into the passage, still hardly able to believe his good luck, not even remotely thinking of danger.

His flat was on the fourth, top floor; like Smith's. The staircase hadn't the same gracious curve, and the doors which led to the other flats were smaller; all of them were painted black. His own was of oak, and solid looking. A thousand times he had come here and found the door opening as he arrived, for Jolly had a sixth sense as to the right moment to expect him. Now, it was hardly likely that the sixth sense was working.

Yet the door began to open. Rollison grinned.

"Oh, no," he said. "Jolly, this is a record. You—"
He broke off.

It was not Jolly at the door; it was a stranger.

.   .   .   .   .

Rollison was close to the door, had been about to stretch out with the key. He was too far away from the stairs to dodge backwards, and even if he had been closer the automatic pistol held in the stranger's right hand would have stopped him. This was the worst moment he had known for a long, long time—and the next was even worse, because another man appeared and came on to the landing.

"Mr. Toff, I presume," he said. He had a hard, English voice.

Rollison said: "The name is Rollison," very quietly. "If you've hurt my man—"

"Jolly's not hurt enough to worry about," said the man by his side; he dropped a hand on Rollison's wrist, and thrust him forward, while the first man backed into the lounge hall of the flat. "No one's going to be hurt if you answer a few simple questions." He kept his hold on Rollison's arm, then with a dexterous twist, thrust it up behind Rollison so that sharp pain shot through his arm and shoulder. "But if we have any difficulty, you'll both get badly hurt."

"You know," Rollison said, "I could shout for the police."

"You could get shot in the belly."

"Then you wouldn't get the answers you're so eager about, would you?" asked Rollison. He stared into the face of the first man, who was not unlike Simon Shawn in build and colouring, but seemed to have much more strength. There were pale blue eyes, a rather hungry look, very thin lips. He had made no attempt to disguise himself, nor had the second stranger, who was smaller and more wiry, who was an expert at that hammerlock, and might be an expert at a lot of others. The pressure on Rollison's arm was so great that it was difficult not to gasp with pain; but he kept silent, and even managed to look relaxed.

"You won't shout for help and you'll answer our questions," the larger man said. "Don't make a fuss about it, Toff. We know all about you and your reputation—in fact we've been admiring your Trophy Wall. Jolly gave us chapter and verse about some of the 'Trophies'." He went into the room beyond, a large living-room with a dining alcove and, in one corner, a large walnut desk, beautifully figured. Along the deak on the wall was a remarkable array of "trophies". Many an astonished visitor had asked if Rollison had robbed Scotland Yard's Museum, for every imaginable kind of lethal weapon was here, each a souvenir from one of Rollison's cases.

Rollison didn't give that a thought.

Jolly was sitting at his desk, tied to his chair, with sticking plaster stuck over his lips—as Shawn had been. At a rakish angle on his head was a top hat with a bullet hole in it, taken from the highest peg on the Trophy Wall. The rope binding him was the most famous of the Toff's souvenirs, a hangman's rope, and the noose was dropped neatly round Jolly's shoulders. His eyes were very bright and huge and frightened.

The bigger man said: "We won't hurt you if you talk quickly, but if you don't, we can start work on Jolly first. We're not playing for peanuts, and we need to know the answers."

Rollison said: "So you do," very softly.

He had no illusions at all. These men were killers.
They had made no attempt to disguise themselves, they
knew he was an expert in giving descriptions, and that it
was virtually certain that if they let him go alive he would
give that description to the police as soon as he could
speak. He reminded himself of the ruthlessness shown so
far: Shawn, Smith, the woman, possibly Dangerfield. No
matter what they said, once they believed that they had
all the information they could get they would kill. It was
easy to imagine them tightening that rope round Jolly's
neck. Judging from his expression, Jolly had the same
kind of pre-vision.

"Listen, Toff," the spokesman said, "we haven't much
time. Did you talk to Gabby Smith tonight?"

Rollison didn't answer.

"Friend," said the smaller man, and increased the
pressure of the hammerlock; the pain at elbow and
shoulder was agonising.

"Did you talk to Gabby?" the first man asked levelly.

"No," answered Rollison. The pressure became even
greater, his body thrust forward and he knew that any
moment a bone might snap; and he was quite sure that
the men would have no compunction.

"Supposing you don't lie," said the bigger man.

Rollison said between his teeth: "Would you know the
difference between a lie and the truth? I followed Smith
from the hotel after he'd collected his wife's clothes." He
paused, saw the man frown as if half-convinced, and went
on: "I traced him to the Rue Morot, and if I'd had any
sense I would have gone straight after him, but I thought
it would be better to have a look round first, so I gave
him time to go to bed. When I got back he was dead."

Half way through this, the big man began to smile.

"All right, Rollison, I believe you," he said. "Lay off, Mick." The pressure at Rollison's arm and wrist eased; there was ache but not acute pain. "Keep on telling the truth and you'll die happy," the speaker went on. "Did you look round his apartment?"

"Yes."

"What did you find?"

"He's a good engraving artist—like Shawn."

"My, my," said the big man, still smiling. "When you let your hair down you let it down, don't you? If you'd taught your man to tell the truth, too, he probably wouldn't be feeling so uncomfortable." He didn't glance at Jolly, but Rollison did, and at that moment the wiry man was hidden from Jolly by Rollison's breadth of shoulder. For the first time an expression appeared in Jolly's eyes; he was trying to convey some kind of message.

And he *winked*.

Rollison's heart leapt, for it was not often that Jolly winked, obviously he was trying to offer reassurance. What possible justification could there be? The only certain thing was that Jolly had a good reason; he was not by nature unduly optimistic.

The big man said: "So you know about Benoit, Shawn and Smith. Being the Toff, the great detective, what brilliant deductions have you made?"

"They don't have to be brilliant," Rollison said, and saw Jolly's eyes swivel towards the star-shaped Regency clock over the mantelpiece. Jolly couldn't move his lips, could hardly move his body, so his eyes had to do all the work. It was now five minutes to seven. Rollison was trying desperately to guess what Jolly meant as he went on: "You've got English, French and American currency ready for issuing, and specialists working on new blocks."

"Isn't he good?" jeered the big man. "What put you on to Benoit, Toff?"

"Now that's easy," Rollison said promptly. "An aunt of mine . . ."

As he told the story of Alice Day's two hundred pounds he expected the big man to call him a liar. Instead the man scowled heavily and said sourly:

"Benoit always was a bloody fool. He must have taken some of the slush and got rid of it on the side. Anyway, you've guessed that this is an international forgery organization."

"Yes."

"How right you are," the big man said, "and what a pity you are, too. It's far too big a scheme to let a life or two stand in the way. It's almost a pity that the great Toff has to go, but better you than I. You didn't talk to Benoit, and he doesn't know enough to matter. Shawn could have talked much more but he won't, now, will he? Gabby Smith pinched him to death. Gabby could have given you a lead to me and to others, but he and his wife are probably having an indignant conference with Shawn wherever bad men go when they're dead. You really haven't discovered anything, Rollison."

Rollison said bleakly: "Not enough."

"This is where you ask me to see reason, where you point out that it's dangerous to commit murder in the heart of London, that when the police discover your body they'll be as mad as if one of their own men had been killed," declared the big man. "You may be right, but some risks have to be taken, Toff. I don't suppose you thought you would come to quite such a quick end." He took the automatic pistol from his pocket, then a short length of rubber; Rollison recognised the silencer, knew that once that was fitted the shot would make little or no noise.

He did not believe that anything would make this man relent. The grey eyes had a bleakness, a hardness, which told of the professional killer. The rubber snout was slipped on to the stubby barrel of the pistol with the smoothness of long practice. The automatic was raised quite casually.

The hands of the clock pointed to seven.

Jolly began to struggle violently, scraping his chair along the carpet, banging his knees against the edge of the desk, but the man with the automatic just glanced at him and said: "Don't make a fuss." Rollison saw the gun pointing at his chest; not his head, which might have given him a chance to duck. The small man held him so that it was impossible to move his body.

There was a split second between him and death.

Then a door banged in the kitchen, far out of sight, and a man called out in a rich Cockney voice:

"Show a leg, Jolly me lad, show a leg!"

13

STEP NEARER

ROLLISON saw the big man's eyes swivel towards the sound, saw the muzzle of the gun waver and droop, felt the momentary relaxation of the smaller man's grip. He shouted: *"Careful there, armed thieves!"* and kicked the smaller man in the shin and leapt at the bigger man. The gun jolted and steadied, and the hand seemed enormous, the forefinger squeezed. Rollison was half way towards the man, a little towards one side. He felt a tug at his shoulder as a bullet went through the jacket padding, then struck the other bodily. He bellowed: *"There are two of them!"* and lurched forward as the big man stumbled backwards, gun arm waving, obviously trying desperately to get it under control. Rollison rammed his clenched right fist into the man's stomach, and as the blond head was jerked forward, placed his hand over the face and hurled the man back. He went staggering, came up against the wall, cracked his head against it, and slumped down.

A man appeared in the doorway carrying a broom.

Rollison stretched out for the automatic, wrenched it free, and swung round towards the little man; but this man was not armed with a gun, all he had was a flick knife. He stood undecided, Rollison with the gun on one side, and the man in the doorway with the broom on the other. The newcomer was small and wiry, too; he wore a cloth cap set at a jaunty angle, a black and white choker, and a bright yellow waistcoat but no jacket. He held the broom in front of him like a battering ram, and lunged forward. The man with the knife dodged to one side, but did not dodge fast enough. The broom whacked into his stomach, and he gasped as he went staggering back. He thudded against the wall, and the little man pressed the head of the broom hard against him. Rollison went across without haste, and took the knife from his hand. Then he went across to Jolly.

"Percy, you will never know how glad I was to see you," he said. "Two minutes later, and you would have found Jolly and me ready for the morgue."

"Let me knock his bloody block orf," pleaded the man with the broom. His name was Wrightson, and he was "one of Ebbutt's men". Jolly had known that he was due at seven o'clock, of course, and that he had a back door key; hence the wink which had brought the birth of hope.

"Just spoil his breakfast for a few days," Rollison said, and put the keen blade of the knife to the hempen rope which bound Jolly. The blade was not only razor sharp but had the point of a dagger. Before he began to cut, Jolly started violently, and Rollison backed away.

"Did I hurt you?"

Jolly shook his head and rolled his eyes. Rollison wiped the sweat off his own forehead, and wondered if Jolly was feeling light-headed. He put the knife forward again, and Jolly shook his head even more violently.

Then he squinted down at the rope.

Rollison said suddenly: "I get you!" and laughed, for Jolly did not want him to cut this rope, which was so exceptional a souvenir. "We'll cut it," he said quietly, "and you shall splice it again with your own fair hands, making two trophies in one."

He studied the way the rope was twisted, and saw that

there was really only one knot, besides that making the
noose. He cut close to this knot, and began to unwind the
rope. It had bitten deeply into Jolly's wrists and ankles,
and now and again his man gasped with pain, but soon
he was completely free.

"Better stay there for a bit," Rollison advised, and
turned round. "I'll get that adhesive plaster off."

Percy Wrightson had simply knocked the smaller of the
two men unconscious, and was now sitting on an upright
chair with the head of the broom close to the bigger man,
who was on the floor. This man's eyes were open, he
looked all right, but he couldn't get up without being
jabbed painfully in the face. Rollison went into the
bathroom. He felt limp, for the shadow of death had
been so very near. He rinsed his hands and face in cold
water, dabbed them dry, and took a small bottle of
surgical spirit from the first aid cabinet. He dabbed the
adhesive plaster on Jolly's mouth with this, and Jolly
caught his breath, almost choked as the fumes went up
his nostrils.

"Won't be long," Rollison assured him, and after a
few seconds began to pluck at a corner; it was still stuck
hard. "Better leave it for a minute or two," he said, and
sat on the desk and began to massage Jolly's wrists.
Jolly looked very pale, but his eyes were bright and alert.
After he had rubbed each wrist briskly, Rollison picked
off the adhesive plaster; it came away easily now.

When Jolly was completely free, he began to work his
lips as if he couldn't speak soon enough.

"Take it easy for a bit," Rollison advised. "After that
near one we can afford to waste a bit of time." He sat on
a corner of the desk, looking down at the big man, and his
expression was harsh and bleak. His right hand moved to
a drawer, he opened it and turned off a switch which

controlled a tape-recorder, specially fitted to keep a report of interviews which might be better on the record. He remembered the tape-recorder at his hotel, but did not let that thought distract him.

"Ever known a better case of justifiable homicide, Percy?" he asked.

"Who's dead?" inquired Percy.

"That chap might be, soon."

"Oh, you'd get away with that all right," Percy said. He had a small, lined face, and although he looked in the forties he was in fact in the thirties, a retired lightweight boxer who had often served the Toff and acted as stand-in for Jolly. "I could give an eye witness report of how you were having a struggle and the gun went off and caught him—where do you think would hurt most, Mr. Ar?"

"We must check in Gray's *Anatomy*," Rollison said. He went forward, bent over the man, and was vividly reminded of Katherine Dangerfield emptying Shawn's pocket. This man made a foolish effort to strike him, and Rollison simply took his head between his hands, and banged it on the floor. The man's eyes rolled.

"That's the spirit," Percy approved. "No messing abaht, that's what I always liked about you, Mr. Ar."

Rollison emptied the man's pockets before he came round, and then straightened up. Jolly was standing in front of the desk, and beginning to move, his face set and pain-racked as the blood began to run through his wrists and ankles again. Rollison went across to help, and Jolly said in a croaking voice:

"I shall be quite all right, sir. You study those things."

It was probably better to leave him to take care of himself, so Rollison opened a worn pigskin wallet which bulged with papers, none of which was as dog-eared as those that had been in Gabriel Smith's pockets. Letters were still in their envelopes, with a book of stamps, a folded handkerchief, two small envelopes, both sealed and obviously containing some kind of tablets. Rollison handled everything cautiously, so that his own prints would not show on them, put the tablets aside, and then read the letters.

They were all addressed to:

Claude Dangerfield Esq.,
10, Mitten Mews, W.1.

The driving licence and the insurance cover note were in the name of Claude Dangerfield, too; and the initials CD were on the handkerchief. The man himself was sitting up against the wall, still under the jabbing threat of Wrightson's broom. As he stared at Rollison, his eyes were narrowed and shiny, his lips were set tightly, his whole attitude was one of frustrated fury. Rollison opened the letters. All were personal, and appeared to have nothing at all to do with the forged banknotes; two were from women, two from men. Nothing in the wallet connected this Dangerfield with the forged currency case, except possibly an envelope in which an air ticket from Paris to London had been kept; the date and time were pencilled on the outside. Claude Dangerfield had flown back from Paris at eleven o'clock last night. The envelope was over-printed:

New World Travel Association.
Luxury Travel at Popular Prices.

Rollison took one of the smaller envelopes, slit it open, shook out two small white tablets, and said:

"I'll take over, Percy. You mix a couple of these with water, and give Mr. Dangerfield the mixture." He was staring at Dangerfield, and saw the sudden glint of apprehension in his eyes, and the way his lips tightened. Jolly was moving about more freely, and drew nearer to Rollison. Percy went out, Rollison stood over Danger-field, and said: "Get up, Claude." When the man didn't move, Rollison thrust out a hand, nipped his nostrils tightly, and heaved upwards. "Get up you murdering son of a beast," he said savagely. "Get up!" Dangerfield scrambled wildly to his feet, and Rollison let him go. "Did you kill Shawn?"

"No," Dangerfield muttered. "Gabby Smith did that job. I told you so."

"On your orders?"

Dangerfield moistened his lips, glanced towards the door from which Wrightson was coming, and said: "Yes." He tried to keep his eyes off Wrightson, who came forward stirring the tablet in the water briskly, but his gaze kept flickering towards the Cockney.

"Did you poison Smith and his wife?"

"She—she wasn't his wife, she was his mistress," Dangerfield said. Now he couldn't keep his eyes off Wrightson, who was standing menacingly by.

"Hope it tastes 'orrible," he announced.

"You'd be surprised how horrible it is," said Rollison. "Don't taste it, you fool!" Percy had raised the cup to his lips, but he snatched it away again. "Did you poison Smith and the woman who lived with him?" Rollison asked Dangerfield.

"Yes."

"Why?"

"I didn't trust them not to talk once you started on them."

"Is that the only reason?"

Dangerfield said thickly: "If I tell you the truth, will you give me a break?"

"If you tell me the truth I won't pour this poison down your gullet," Rollison said, and the savage note was harsh in his voice. "If you lie, I'll make you drink it, and explain to the police that you preferred to commit suicide than be charged with murder."

"*Poison?*" echoed Percy, and thrust the cup out at arm's length. "Strewth, an' I nearly 'ad a mouthful. Mr. Ar, the *smell* won't do me no harm, will it? I had a n'efty sniff while I was in the kitchen."

"The odour won't hurt you, Percy," Rollison assured him. "It will kill you in an hour or so if you swallow a mouthful, that's all. Won't it, Claude?" The "Claude" had a savage edge to it, a kind of harsh flippancy. "What was the other reason for murdering Smith?"

"He—he'd finished the job we wanted him for," answered Dangerfield, hoarsely. He tried to edge away from Rollison, as if the cold glint in Rollison's eyes frightened him. "I'm telling you the truth, aren't I?"

"Keep at it," Rollison urged. "So you killed Smith and his mistress because they'd finished their job. Is that why you killed Shawn?"

"Y-yes, partly. He knew a lot more, he could have blown the whole thing wide open."

"Well, well," said Rollison. "And instead of Shawn, you're going to blow the gaff as it's never been blown before. If you don't, I shall pinch your nose again, and Percy will pour that muck down your throat."

"Mr. Ar—" Percy began, uneasily.

"I hope I may have that privilege, sir," said Jolly, and took the cup away from Percy Wrightson. His hand was quite steady, although his wrists were red and swollen, still showing the marks of the rope.

"For God's sake take the stuff away!"

"What is the poison?" Rollison demanded.

Dangerfield drew a hawking breath. "Curare," he said, thinly. "It will kill within an hour. I'll tell you all I know, but there are a lot of facts I don't know, Rollison. I can't tell you what I don't know!"

Sweat was standing out on his forehead, and the veins were standing out on his neck. Just as Rollison had been sure that he would kill, so he seemed sure that Rollison would not hesitate to kill him.

How much could he be made to tell?

14

QUESTIONS AND ANSWERS

JOLLY moved about a little as Rollison asked questions. Percy Wrightson backed to the big desk and leaned on it. Claude Dangerfield stood leaning against the wall heavily, as if he were close to a state of collapse. His face very pale and his eyes feverishly bright; Rollison remembered the way that Katherine Dangerfield had looked just before she had fainted after Shawn's body had been found.

Claude and Katherine—and Alec; all Dangerfields.

Rollison opened the drawer and switched on the tape-machine as he asked: "How did you kill Smith and the woman?"

"I have a key to their apartment, I knew they always had coffee in the evening, I've often stayed there. I ground up two tablets and mixed them with the coffee—the coffee was already in the percolator, ready to go on the stove."

"Did Smith engrave dollar plates for you?"

"Yes."

"And Benoit, French francs?"

"French and Belgian, yes. Roll—Rollison—"

"Shawn did English notes?"

"Yes."

"What other countries are affected?"

"About—" Dangerfield half closed his eyes, almost as if he were frightened of the result of his admission. "About ten."

"European?"

"Yes."

"How is the distribution done?"

Dangerfield said, hurriedly: "That's one of the things I don't know. Rollison, it's no use looking like that, I don't know! There are three different departments—the art work and engraving, the printing and the distributing. I helped to organise the artwork, I don't know anything about the rest."

Rollison glanced at Jolly.

"Believe him, Jolly?"

"No, sir."

"For God's sake! It's the truth!"

"Leave it for the moment," Rollison said, "but don't make any mistake, Dangerfield, we can pour this stuff down your throat, and when the pathologist opens you up and finds the dope—the curare—I shall tell him that you swallowed a couple of tablets when I wasn't looking. Don't kid yourself that I'd have any qualms. Are you Alec Dangerfield's brother?"

"Yes," this man muttered.

"Where is he?"

"That's—that's another thing I don't know," Dangerfield said. "I can't give you information that I don't know."

"You needn't labour the point, I'll decide whether you're telling the truth or not," Rollison said. "Is he alive?"

"I—I believe so."

"Not sure?"

"No."

"So you'd allow your bosses to murder your own brother, would you?"

"There isn't anything I could do about it!"

"You could avenge him."

"Listen, Rollison," Dangerfield said, with a taut earnestness in his manner; he stood up very straight, and stretched out a hand. "I'm in this racket as deep as I can go. I'm in it for what I can get out of it. My brother might get run over by a car or pick up some killer disease, and it wouldn't make any difference to me. If I could save his life without risking my own I'd try, but if they kill him, I can't stop them, and I'm not going to cut my throat trying to cut theirs."

Rollison said to Jolly, coldly: "That much I believe. Have we ever known men worse?"

"I'm sure we haven't, sir."

"All right, so I'm as bad as they come by your standards," Dangerfield said, and now he raised his voice, as if he believed that he could save his life by impassioned pleading. "I've been off-beat for most of my life. If my precious brother had lifted a finger to help me fifteen years ago, probably this would never have happened, but all I got from him were pennies and prayers, the righteous humbug. He—" Sweat was dripping down Dangerfield's forehead and cheeks and into his eyes, but there could be little doubt that he was telling the truth about the family relationship. "So I hated his guts. I got him into this, I laid it all on. We needed some top-line artists and engravers, there wasn't a better man to find them, and he did it all right. He thought we wanted them for a special high-class book printing job, he didn't know what they were really wanted for, but the fool found out. They couldn't leave him in circulation then, they had to take him away. I—I think he's alive. I—I don't think they'll kill him if he'll promise to keep quiet about it."

"Will he promise?"

"If he won't it's his own bloody fault."

"Will he?" asked Rollison, more softly.

"I doubt it," Dangerfield said, in a choky voice. "He's the kind of imbecile who would die for a principle. I told him if he laid low he needn't worry, he could have had a big cut in the profits, but he was going to Scotland Yard. You know that as well as I do."

"Yes, I know," said Rollison, but in fact he did not know at all. Now he had to find out why Dangerfield thought that he knew, without letting the man realise what he was doing.

"He'd have gone straight there if I hadn't worked on him," Dangerfield said. "I sold him the line that I was going to break the racket up, and that kept him away from the Yard, but he had to come and see you."

Rollison said, softly: "So that's why he came to see me."

"You know damned well that's why!"

"No," said Rollison. "He was a better brother than you knew. He didn't tell me anything about you, he just told me he thought his artists were being used for forgery," Rollison said slowly, but his mind was working very fast, as he tried to understand the full implications of all this. Dangerfield believed that his brother Alec had come to see him, believed that he knew more than he did, and there was no need to disabuse him yet. "Why wait until now to keep me quiet?" he demanded.

The man answered: "We were watching you in London, and you didn't get on to Shawn or any of the other artists, so Alec couldn't have told you much. It wasn't until you went to Paris and started watching Benoit that we really realised you were closer than we thought."

"So it wasn't," Rollison said. He turned round to look at Percy Wrightson, but Percy had vanished. The odour of frying bacon floated into the room, so Percy had broken one of Jolly's primary rules: always close the kitchen door while cooking. Jolly was still sitting close by Rollison's side.

Rollison went on: "Where's your brother, Dangerfield?"

"I've told you I don't know!" The harsh voice rose. "I've told you everything I can, it's no use asking me."

"Believe him now, Jolly?" inquired Rollison.

"Not for one moment, sir."

"Watch him, will you?" said Rollison, and turned and went into the kitchen. There Percy Wrightson was standing over the gas stove, prodding sausages lovingly; the bacon was in another frying pan, already beautifully golden and crisp.

"Don't leave it too long, Mr. Ar," Wrightson pleaded. "I've got a n'appetite like a n'orse."

"Have yours, Percy, and cook more for us if we're late," said Rollison. He opened a glass cupboard, took out a cup identical with the one in which the curare tablets had been mixed, put in a little water and stirred in some baking powder; the resulting mixture looked like the one in the other cup. He winked at Wrightson, who gave the thumbs-up sign before turning a sausage over to its under-done side. Rollison put the mixture on a table close to the door of the big room, and went back inside. Jolly and Dangerfield were staring at each other like cat and mouse, and Dangerfield's gaze shifted to Rollison only for a moment.

"Has he talked any more yet?" Rollison asked mildly.

"No, sir."

"There's nothing else I can tell you!"

"Name the other artists," Rollison ordered.

"Yes, I can do that, you didn't ask me that before. They're all over the place, but their addresses are in

Alec's office, and I've got copies at my flat. It's no use asking me to give their addresses from memory. I don't know them all."

"Name the men."

"Benoit, Carter, Fairweather, Gregg-Watson, Johnston, Masterton . . ."

"You can write them down when we've finished, if you can write anything," Rollison said in that same bleak voice. "Where's your brother?"

"I tell you I don't even know whether he's alive or dead!"

"Name your Boss."

"Rollison, I can't, you know I can't. You know—"

"Name him."

"I can't name him! In any case I don't really know him, I only deal through a kind of contact man, a liaison officer, this is too big for anyone to know everything. If they ever find out that I've told you all this—"

"They won't pay your defence, is that it?" sneered Rollison. "You know them and you're going to name them." He motioned to Jolly, who picked up the poison cup. New dread flared up in Dangerfield's eyes, and he did exactly what Rollison expected: he struck out at the cup, trying to upset the contents. Jolly pulled it back out of reach, and Rollison rammed his elbow into the man's stomach, bringing an *ooch* of pain, and knocking him back against the wall. Rollison took the cup, went to the door and switched cups, and was back before Dangerfield had recovered and while the tears were still streaming from his eyes. It was several minutes before the tears stopped, and even then he was half doubled up. He stared at the cup now in Jolly's hand, convinced that it was a drink of death.

"Name your Boss," Rollison ordered coldly.

"I—I swear I don't know!"

"I swear I'll make you drink this if you don't tell me," Rollison said, in the same icy voice.

"You—you'd never do it." The words screeched.

"You're pushing me hard," Rollison said, and the look on his face as well as the tone of his voice gave no indication of mercy. He called: "Percy!"

After a moment, Wrightson appeared; chewing.

"Come and put a lock on Dangerfield," said Rollison.

"Arf a mo'," said Wrightson. He gulped energetically then strode purposefully across the long room. "Rather break his neck, Mr. Ar, but your way's probably the best." When Dangerfield tried to get away Wrightson feinted with his right, then with his left, but almost at the same time he caught the man's right wrist, twisted, and thrust his arm behind him, exactly as the other man had worked on Rollison half an hour earlier. "Okay, Mr. Ar?"

"Fine," said Rollison. "I'll make him open his mouth, Jolly. Percy, don't forget that he swallowed those tablets of his own free will, it's been done often enough before." He took the helpless man's nose between his thumb and forefinger, and Dangerfield was compelled to open his mouth wide. Jolly stepped forward, ready to pour the liquid down.

Dangerfield was writhing and trying to struggle, and trying to shout. It was impossible to make out what he said, and Rollison let him go, stood back, waited for a moment, and then said:

"What did you say?"

"I'll tell you all I can," gasped Dangerfield. "I'll tell you who I work through, I can't name the boss, all I know about him is that he owns a big travel agency. The man I work through is Marvin Oliver, Betty Oliver's brother. They—they both work at Alec's agency. I swear that's all I can tell you, but Oliver knows the boss, he knows whether my brother's alive." Dangerfield was gabbling, almost sobbing. "For God's sake don't give me that stuff."

Rollison said: "We'll check with this Marvin Oliver first. Does his sister know anything about it?"

"I don't think so, but I'm not sure. That's the truth, Rollison, it's the absolute truth..'

"All right, Percy," Rollison said. "We'll let him go. March him over to that cupboard next to the spare room, he can commune with himself there." He watched Dangerfield being frogmarched across the room and Jolly, moving with reasonable freedom, going after them.

As they reached the door, Rollison called:

"Dangerfield!"

All three of them stopped, and Dangerfield tried to turn his head.

"What is Oliver's address?"

"He has a flat in Mountain Street, not far from here."

"What number?"

"Thirty-one, on the top floor."

"Right," said Rollison, and nodded to Wrightson, who thrust the prisoner forward again. Before they were out of sight, Rollison went to the telephone standing on the corner of his desk, lifted the receiver and dialled a White-chapel number. The ringing sound seemed to go on for a long time, but before Jolly or Wrightson was back, a man said gruffly:

"Ebbutt speaking, whossat?"

"Bill, I've another urgent job for you," Rollison said. "Send a couple of lively chaps to a man named Marvin Oliver at thirty-one Mountain Street, off Berkeley Square, and see that no harm comes to him. One back, one front, and hold him until I arrive if you can. If you can't, just follow him. This might be the day with his name on it."

"I'll fix it, Mr. Ar," said Ebbutt, in a richer, deeper Cockney than Wrightson's; he was a deeper, bigger man in every respect. "You okay?"

"Thanks to Percy. I shall have a special gold medal struck for him."

"He bin useful?" asked Ebutt, highly gratified. "That's the ticket. I say, you've put up a beauty this time, Mr. Ar. That Mrs. D.'s knocked my boys right over, and it ain't only with statistics. Had a report from the Marigold Club late last night, no trouble of any kind, and if there's been any during the night I'd 'eard by now. Okay, Mr. Ar . . . 'ere, 'old on!" There was a pause before Ebbutt came back on the line, and Rollison was quite sure that he was grinning broadly. "S'nothing," he declared. 'Lil send her regards, that's all." He rang off with a wheezy chuckle. Rollison replaced the receiver, smiling, and as it went *ting*! heard the front door bell.

That was unusual at twenty-five minutes to eight in the morning.

He turned towards the door leading to the entrance hall, crossed quickly, but was not as quick as Jolly, who had travelled via the domestic quarters, and was looking up at the small periscope-type mirror fastened above the front door, making it possible to see callers without their knowing they were being watched. That had been one of Jolly's brighter ideas, for Claude Dangerfield had not been the first caller who had come with ill-intent.

Rollison waited for word from Jolly, who turned his head and mouthed:

"*Superintendent Grice.*"

"He's had word from Corbin," Rollison told himself, and beckoned Jolly, who tip-toed towards him. "Get

Dangerfield's pal out of the living-room. You and Percy hold him until I give the word." They were already in the big room. "Is Grice by himself?"

"As far as I could see, sir, but he knows we have the mirror and may have instructed a man to stay out of range. Is there any need to be anxious?"

"It wouldn't surprise me a bit," said Rollison, and as he and Jolly bent down to get Dangerfield's accomplice to his feet, there was a much longer ring at the front door bell.

15

GRICE

Superintendent William Grice was a tall, well built man, but bony and on the lean side. He was dressed now, as usually, in a well-cut suit of brown, and he might even be called a brown man, for his complexion was sallow, his eyes were brown, and where the grey hadn't yet taken possession, his hair was the colour of a chestnut gelding. He had a hooked nose and across the bridge the skin was stretched very tightly, so that it seemed white; and on the left side of his face, mostly under the chin, was an ugly scar. That was a reminder of a wound caused by an explosion in which he and the Toff had nearly been killed.

These men had worked sometimes as adversaries and often together for twenty years, and now they were close friends. But Grice was first and last a policeman, like Corbin, and when the Toff came into conflict with the law, Grice came sharply into conflict with the Toff. His expression as he stepped into the room suggested he wasn't feeling well-disposed, and he didn't speak as Rollison led him into the living-room.

In the three minutes while Grice had been waiting, the Toff, Jolly and Wrightson had worked miracles. There was no trace of the trouble here, the top hat had been slung into position on its peg, and only the hangman's rope was missing from its usual place, curled up inside a drawer.

"I repeat," said Rollison mildly, "good morning, William."

Grice said: "I always told you that one day you would lose what little common sense you ever had. Now you've lost it. I've got Corbin over from Paris. He's made a list of charges as long as my arm. He's storming for an extradition warrant, too, and as two of the charges are murder, he'll get it. Why didn't you take my advice and be careful?"

"But I didn't kill anyone," protested Rollison.

"I'm not so sure."

"Aren't you?" asked Rollison, sadly. He went behind his desk, opened the tape recorder drawer wide enough to get his hand inside, but did not switch it on, although the tape was all ready to play back. "Sit down, Bill."

"I didn't come here for a social chat. I want to know if you've any defence at all against these charges. That you suffocated Simon Shawn. That you broke into an apartment belonging to an American citizen named Gabriel Smith. That you poisoned Smith and his mistress, assaulted a policeman, and used a false passport to get out of France. Also that you accused a man named Benoit of stealing your wallet, when in fact you put the wallet in his pocket." Grice paused, and then growled: "Well? Any two of these charges are enough to make sure you're taken back to Paris under escort."

"Corbin's certainly thrown the book at me," said Rollison, still mildly, but there was an edge to his voice. "All the answers, of course, are no, no, no, not guilty, not guilty, not guilty—how many times is that?"

"This isn't a joking matter," Grice rasped.

Rollison's expression sharpened. "No," he said. "It isn't a laughing matter, either. I'm not sure who's the bigger idiot, you or Corbin. Corbin knows what this is all about and lets his injured dignity get the better of him, while you ought to know that I might conceivably have suffocated a man by accident but certainly didn't poison anyone."

"The charge is made, and—"

"You could have used a different approach," Rollison interrupted, with the note of acerbity sharp in his voice. "You could have said: 'Rolly, I know there's an explanation but you're in a hell of a spot. Is there anything I can do to get you out of it?' Instead you prefer to come storming in as if you were dealing with an old lag."

"That's quite enough," Grice said. "I've a warrant for your arrest in my pocket. Unless you can offer positive proof that the charges are unjustified, I shall execute it."

Rollison said bleakly: "All right, go ahead and execute it. Take me back to Paris. Let me stew in a French jail. And when you've been ridiculed by every newspaper in England and Corbin's been demoted for making a bumptious fool of himself, don't say I didn't warn you. My God, I—"

"*Good*-morning, Mr. Grice," greeted Jolly. He came into the room carrying a silver tray, coffee, toast, butter and marmalade. "I'm very glad to see you again." Jolly smiled serenely upon the Yard man, and Rollison had never heard his voice more suave. "I thought you might care for some coffee. I know Mr. Rollison must be famished. He hasn't slept all night, he had considerable exertions in Paris as you may possibly know, and such an unpleasant reception here. I suppose it's impracticable, but I would be much happier if it were possible for you to question him after he has rested for an hour or so. After all, a man who has been within an ace of losing his life can't really be expected to—"

"Enough oil, Jolly," Rollison interrupted.

"I beg your pardon, sir?"

"Mr. Grice was making a fool of himself, and I don't want you to apologise for me because I was just as bad."

"I do beg your pardon, sir," said Jolly, still sweetly. "I wonder if you would care to have breakfast—full breakfast I mean—immediately, or whether this will be sufficient?"

"This will be sufficient."

"Very good, sir."

"Well, it's not sufficient for me, guv'nor," Percy Wrightson announced from the doorway. He came in with his yellow waistcoat partly hidden by an apron, his wiry gingery hair standing straight up from his head, his thin and lined cheeks spotted with scarlet. "It's abaht time someone tore a strip orf you, Gricey, and I'm just the one to do it. Bin looking forward to it for twenty years, I have, ever since you was a sooty nosed little bas—"

"That is quite enough." Jolly's voice lost its sweet reasonableness.

"Don't you lay your pansy hands on me," Wrightson barked, and shook himself free. "This streak of skin and bone who calls himself a police superintendent—why, I've eaten bigger things than him before breakfast. Why the hell don't they get some coppers with intelligence instead of bloody big feet, that's what I want to know. You come in here talking to Mr. Rollison knowing flickin' well he's worth twenty coppers rolled into one—and by Gawd, he can prove it!" Percy swung round and pointed to the trophy wall. "Take me to *your* office, Gricey. Show me how many jobs you've handled with your own fair hands. Why, the Toff's done more singlehanded than the whole flicking Flying Squad put together, more than every super at the Yard put together, more than—"

Grice turned towards the wall, as if willed to do so; and exclaimed:

"Where's the rope?"

"Eh?" ejaculated Wrightson. "What rope?"

"The hangman's rope," said Grice, and looked searchingly at Rollison. "Where is it?"

"Lars time I saw it it was round Jolly's scraggy neck, if I 'adn't come when I did you'd 'ave 'im strung up, and Mr. Ar with a couple of bullets in his belly. I suppose what you would 'ave done then was fly 'is cawpuss over to Paris. Charter a special airplane, that's what you'd do, stick a few flowers on the coffin and send it to the French narks with your compliments. Why you make me——"

Rollison was leaning back, looking at him and smiling; and glancing sideways at Grice, who was now completely relaxed, all bad humour gone.

"Pack it in, Percy," Jolly said, so colloquially and so unexpectedly that Wrightson gaped at him.

"Thanks, Percy," Rollison said warmly. "Our Bill and I are feeling a lot better. It does everyone good to blow off a bit of steam. Thanks."

"Well, if you're sure——"

"Just what happened here?" Grice asked.

Rollison explained as Jolly poured coffee, Wrightson stood in the doorway attentively, and Grice listened closely. Grice didn't once interrupt or shift his position. Jolly placed coffee in front of each of them, and went out, reluctantly. Wrightson also went to the kitchen, out of earshot. As he drew near the end of the story, Rollison switched on the tape-recorder to play it back, and a humming sound made a background to his voice until soon the conversation which he had had with Claude Dangerfield was repeated. Drinking coffee, eating toast and marmalade, and contemplating each other they listened intently. Rollison leaned forward and switched off at the point where Dangerfield had told him of Marvin Oliver's address.

"And I had Bill Ebbutt send two men to try and make sure Oliver doesn't run into trouble," Rollison said.

"Why not the police instead of Ebbutt?" asked Grice.

"Because I thought you'd probably take too much time checking why I wanted Oliver watched," answered Rollison, "and because I would prefer to talk to Oliver myself without him knowing that the police were on his tail. I'm old-fashioned enough to think that he might talk to me and not to you, because he will think he might be able to do a deal with me."

"You could be right," Grice conceded. "I'll take that tape with me, and when the Assistant Commissioner's heard it he'll tell Corbin that he can have a duplicate tape but he can't have you. Sorry I lost my temper, Rolly, but I had asked you nicely, and this could have become an international incident. The head of the Sûreté Nationale telephoned the Commissioner, and that really started things boiling. When I came here you were so damned smug."

"Sorry, too," murmured Rollison. "I did ask for it, and Jolly's right, I need a few hours with my head down." He smiled faintly. "As usual the trouble is that I will never trust anyone else to do a job. You know the feeling."

Grice said: "Yes. The amazing thing is—" and broke off.

"That forged currency of a dozen or more countries is being distributed, and no one appears to have suspected it," Rollison observed. "If ever Interpol should have a job on its plate, this is it. The whole plot has been brilliantly handled as far as we can judge, Bill, and the leaders have made sure that their top big men really are killers. Have you ever come across Claude Dangerfield before?"

"No."

"Alec Dangerfield?"

"Yes, once," said Grice, slowly. "I met him at the time Shawn was being charged with engraving blocks for making ten shilling notes. Dangerfield put up some of the money for Shawn's defence, but always swore he'd never suspected this under cover work."

"Think he was lying?"

"I know we couldn't prove anything against him at the time. He stood up to questioning, and his affairs stood up to investigation," Grice said. "I remember his wife, too, I met her twice at his office. And I remember his secretary, this Betty Oliver—rather plump, jolly type, the ideal secretary species. I don't remember meeting this Marvin Oliver." He stood up, briskly. "I'll get back to the Yard and talk things over with the A.C. He might agree with me that it would be better to let you have a go at Marvin Oliver first, but you haven't a chance of going to Dangerfield's flat in Mitten Mews before us, you might as well save your time. What about this second man who was with Dangerfield?"

"He's here too, but I don't know what Jolly's done with him."

"Let me use your telephone, will you?" said Grice, and as Rollison pushed it towards him, he dialled the Yard. In a brisk authoritative voice he gave instructions for a police car to come and fetch Claude Dangerfield and the other man, for a team to go to the flat in Mitten Mews and make a thorough search, and for two men to watch Oliver's flat without giving themselves away. Before he rang off, he said: "Hold on a minute," and looked at

Rollison. "Want reinforcements at the Marigold Club to make sure that Mrs. Dangerfield is safe?"

Rollison pursed his lips.

"Not a bad idea," he approved. "Bill Ebbutt will hate me for it, but I can always say that you wouldn't play it my way. I shouldn't let dear Kate know that the police are also watching her."

"All right," Grice said, and picked up the tape recorder. "Pity you didn't bring the one from the hotel in Paris."

"If Corbin's the man I think he is he's had several recordings made from that tape already," said Rollison. "Give him my love."

"He'll probably want to cut your throat," said Grice, and grinned. "As I wanted to, half an hour ago. Thanks for the coffee, and tell Jolly he's gone way up in my estimation. I—"

He broke off as they reached the door leading to the lounge hall, for the front door bell rang. He knew about the periscope mirror and stepped ahead of Rollison so as to see who was there. A moment later Jolly appeared; and at the same moment, Rollison recognised Katherine Dangerfield and another woman. This woman was shorter and plumper, and looked shocked and grief-stricken.

"That," announced Grice, "is Betty Oliver."

16

DEATH BY POISONING

THE small mirror made it difficult to see Katherine Dangerfield as clearly as Marvin Oliver's sister, and in any case she was probably more capable of hiding her feelings. As Jolly opened the door Grice and Rollison went back into the sitting room, Rollison feeling the old familiar pounding of his heart as the obvious possibility came to him that Alec Dangerfield had been found dead.

He would know the moment he saw Katherine face to face.

He heard Jolly murmur, then Katherine Dangerfield's voice, then footsteps. He stood up from his desk as the two women entered. A glance convinced him that this was not bad news about Katherine's husband; the bad news was Betty Oliver's. The obvious meaning of this call came to him with savage force. Disaster had struck Oliver, not Alec Dangerfield. As he greeted Katherine, he reminded himself that two of the main players in this tragic drama were complete strangers to him; he had never met Alec Dangerfield or Oliver.

". . . I'd told Betty my telephone number, I had to talk to her last night," said Katherine, quietly. "This morning she telephoned me with this dreadful news that her brother died during the night."

"It's so awful," Betty Oliver said in a constricted voice. Given colour in her cheeks and without the signs of shock in her eyes, she would have been a happy-looking woman;

as it was, she was quite handsome, and had most beautiful corn-coloured hair and the deepest of cornflower blue eyes. "I spent the evening with him last night, we've always made a habit of spending one evening a week together, ever since our parents died—for fifteen *years*." Her voice fell away to a whisper. "Fifteen years," she repeated as if every syllable hurt her. "He was a bit worried, I thought. He had a telephone call from Paris, and wouldn't say anything to me about it, just said that it wasn't from Katherine. We knew Katherine had gone over to try to see you, Mr. Rollison, she confided in us. I—I thought it was news about Alec, was afraid that Alec was dead, but he wouldn't tell me. Marvin's always tried to protect me ever since—"

She broke off.

Grice said, quite briskly: "Exactly what happened, Miss Oliver? How did you learn about your brother?"

"It was the maid at his flat," explained Betty Oliver, huskily. "He's got a service flat, and he always has morning tea at half-past seven. The maid found him dead this morning, and told the manager of the flats. He telephoned me. I called Katherine, and she met me at the flat. I—I had to see for myself, had to be sure."

"And are you sure?" asked Grice.

"Of course I am," she said.

Tears began to flood her eyes.

"The doctor told us that it was some form of poisoning," announced Katherine Dangerfield. She looked much better than she had the previous day, as if a night's rest had helped her to recover from her own shock. "I think it might be murder, Mr. Rollison." Not Rolly.

"What makes you suggest that?" Grice demanded.

"I know Marvin too well to think he would kill himself," Katherine said, crisply. "I only wish—"

The telephone bell on Rollison's desk began to ring, and although Jolly could answer on an extension Rollison lifted the receiver; he wanted something to break this curious tension, and this was heaven-sent.

"Rollison here," he announced, and everyone looked at him.

"Mr. Ar, I've just 'ad word from my boys at that Mountain Street place," declared Bill Ebbutt, wheezing more than usual. "That chap's a goner, Mr. Ar. S'fack. When my boys got there there was a doctor, a n'ambulance, and Mrs. Dangerfield. Another woman was there, the dead bloke's sister if my boys got it right."

"They got it right, Bill," Rollison said. "Thanks for calling. Keep everything else going as arranged, will you?" He rang off on Ebbutt's: "Sure thing," and looked gravely into Betty Oliver's eyes.

She said: "It's absolutely unthinkable that my brother would kill himself. It must be murder!" The tears were very close to the surface again, and she closed her eyes for a moment. "He's been worried ever since Alec went away. I think he was frightened by that telephone call from Paris. But I can't understand why anyone would frighten him, why—" she broke off.

"We will do everything we can to find out quickly," Grice assured her. "I don't want to make things more difficult than they are, Miss Oliver, but a little later I would like you to make a full statement of everything you know about your brother's friends, his recent movements, any cause he might have for anxiety. And Mrs. Dangerfield, now that the truth about your husband's disappearance is known to us officially, I shall need a similar statement from you."

"I suppose I shall have to give it," Katherine said. She looked at Rollison, her honey-coloured eyes narrowed, and he sensed a mood of acute dislike. "I suppose you *had* to tell the police, Mr. Rollison," she went on coldly. "Presumably you wouldn't have done had it been avoidable." Her eyes seemed to add: "Or would you? Was I wise to trust you?" When Rollison just looked at her, she went on to Grice: "I hope you understand, superintendent, that my husband's life is in jeopardy. If these barbarous people know that you are aware of what has been happening, they may murder him in cold blood—as they appear to have killed Marvin."

"I fully understand the situation," said Grice.

"What are you going to do about it?"

Grice said: "Now I don't think I do understand."

"How are you going to make sure that the men who hold my husband prisoner don't learn of this?"

"There isn't any way of preventing them," Grice said flatly. "They will know that we are investigating the death of Mr. Oliver, they'll be bound to know that we will question you about it, and they'll know that we're not entirely fools, Mrs. Dangerfield. They will realise that we are bound to learn that your husband has been missing for over seven weeks, and will want to find out why. I think you must assume that from now on the men who have taken your husband know that they can't keep the kidnapping quiet any longer." When Katherine didn't answer, just stared at him critically, he went on almost uneasily: "No one can possibly be blamed."

"Can't they?" asked Katherine, flatly. She looked at Rollison and her expression and her voice were cold and distant. "You haven't helped very much, Mr. Rollison, have you?"

Rollison said: "No, Mrs. Dangerfield."

"Mrs. Dangerfield—" Grice began.

"For heaven's sake, what does it matter, if it helps to

find Alec?" Betty Oliver demanded. She had been sitting and staring straight in front of her, and Rollison had studied her, wondering what was passing through her mind. "That's the only possible good that can come out of it—now the police have to investigate, and they might find Alec. I never did like the idea of going to an amateur." She glanced at Rollison, and added quickly: "I don't mean to be unkind, I'm sure you did your best, but I've always doubted whether you could really do anything. I wanted Katherine to go to the police—didn't I, Kate?"

"Yes, Betty," said Katherine quietly, "and I'm beginning to think you were right." She turned from Rollison to Grice. "The only reason I kept away from you was to try to save my husband. I was warned so clearly that if I reported that he was missing, he would be killed. Now—there must be *some* chance that he's alive."

"There *must* be!" echoed Betty Oliver; the tears were beginning to spill down her face.

"Provided you give us all possible information, I think there's a reasonable chance that we will find out soon," Grice said, "but it must be all the information, Mrs. Dangerfield. Will you come straight to Scotland Yard with me now, so that we can talk to you?"

Katherine said sharply: "Now? but Miss Oliver—"

"I'll be all right, Kate," Betty said, and she was obviously trying to keep back tears. "No one will try to hurt me, I'll be all right. Perhaps I can stay here for a little while, until I feel more able to cope."

"For as long as you like," Rollison said.

Katherine Dangerfield looked at him, and her expression seemed to say: "I hope you do better by Betty than you have by me," but she didn't put it into words. She said: "Presumably there's no need for me to stay at the Marigold Club any longer."

"Why don't you let yourself be advised by the police?" suggested Rollison.

"I think I will," said Katherine, coldly.

She went out with Grice, as the police squad arrived to take charge of Claude Dangerfield and his companion. Rollison saw her off. She did not look round from the stairs, but Grice did, and gave a curious kind of grimace, as if he were saying that he knew he had a handful in this woman.

Rollison went thoughtfully back into the living-room, where Betty Oliver was sitting in a large armchair, drinking hot coffee which, he felt sure, had plenty of sugar in it: Jolly knew how to treat shock. Rollison felt a burning at the back of his eyes, worse now that he was able to relax a little. He had been up late that night before, and hadn't closed his eyes for twenty-six hours. He had a curiously jaded feeling, too, because of Katherine Dangerfield's mood of censure, and he hardly needed telling that he hadn't exactly covered himself with glory.

Percy Wrightson appeared in the doorway leading from the kitchen quarters, and said brusquely:

"Told you where to get off, Mr. Ar, didn't she? If I'd been you I'd have given her a good smack on the—"

"Forget it, Percy."

"Nah, I'm not going to forget it," declared Percy Wrightson, and stood facing him aggressively. "What are they all picking on you for? There's that French dick, then there's Grice, if I hadn't slapped him down whose side would *he* have been on?" When Rollison didn't answer, Wrightson went on even more indignantly: "And then that Madame looks at you as if you were dirt. If she'd told you abaht it weeks or even a couple of days ago you'd have had more chance, that's what I say."

"Forget it, Percy," Rollison said.

"You know the trouble with you? You're too soft-'earted, that's wot," declared Wrightson indignantly. "Always trying to see the other man's point of view, that's wot. Like to know something, Mr. Ar? That's a sucker's game. So she expected you to work miracles and you didn't. Is that a crime? Is that—"

Percy Wrightson ran on and on. Jolly was undoubtedly within earshot, and did not attempt to stop the Cockney, so presumably he approved of this line of argument, and there was a lot to be said for it. Rollison sat on the corner of his desk and watched Betty Oliver, who had finished her coffee and was now staring at the Trophy wall, but he doubted whether she noticed any of the individual things on it. She seemed oblivious of what Wrightson was saying, as if it had no interest for her, but quite suddenly she interrupted:

"Mr. Rollison."

"Yes."

"Do you think they'll ever find Alec alive?"

"It isn't any use guessing," Rollison said gently, "but if it's possible, we'll find him."

She said: "I can't stand it if he dies too. I just can't stand it. And now that Marvin's gone there's no one I can talk to, and I've got to talk to someone. That's why I stayed behind, I've got to talk to *you*." Her eyes were feverishly bright as she went on: "The only one who ever knew the real truth was Marvin. He knew that I—I worship Alec. I always have, I've loved him so much. And it was terrible, hiding it from him, hiding it from Kate, hiding it from everyone. And now—now these dreadful things are happening. All Alec's oldest friends are being killed. Marvin—oh, God, I can hardly believe it, but Marvin has worked with him for fifteen years! And Gabby Smith was one of the first artists who had ever let

Alec sell his work. Shawn—Shawn was a favourite of his, too, and Kate always knew Shawn was a brilliant artist. He was a friend of the family really. And they're all being killed."

She paused, and then said huskily: "I wonder if they'll try to kill me next."

17

NO CONTACT?

"BIT tough, that is," declared Percy Wrightson to Jolly twenty minutes later. "Her brother gets knocked orf, and she's nuts on a bloke who might be dead and who's married, anyway. Then she's afraid she'll be knocked orf. Amazing way Mr. Ar has with them, though. Went into the spare room and took that sleeping powder like a lamb, didn't she?"

"She was obviously quite exhausted," Jolly said.

"Talk about being aht on your plates of meat, never seen the Toff tuckered aht so much as he is today," went on Wrightson. They were in Jolly's small workshop; sometimes called a laboratory, and Jolly was putting small quantities of sugar, salt, coffee and other powdered or granulated foods into test tubes, and warming these over Bunsen burners. "Looks as if he could sleep the clock round, but he won't, not a chance. Think he's okay?" Wrightson put down a warm test tube and picked up another, but he looked into Jolly's brown eyes, his own bright blue and intelligent. "Not been overdoing it, has he? The way he went for Gricey wasn't like him. Got the patience of Job, Mr. Ar has, but there was a time when I thought he would knock Gricey's block off. Got over it pretty quick, of course, and so did Gricey, but you see what I mean. Think he needs a rest, Mr. Jolly?"

"That is largely why he went to Paris," Jolly said, removing one test tube and replacing it with another. "He hasn't fully recovered from that extremely bad bout of influenza which he had in March. However, I don't think there is much need to worry."

"Dunno abaht that," said Wrightson. "Never seen him quite so quiet. There's a word for it. Subdood, that's it subdood. That Mrs. D. gave him a kick in the pants and he took it on the chin but didn't like it."

"You haven't seen enough of Mr. Rollison to judge his mood," Jolly said. "Percy, I assure you that Mr. Rollison is thinking a great deal. He is subdued, as you say, because he wants to try to assess the situation from every possible angle. You made an ill-informed remark not long ago, criticising his habit of feeling for other people. That is part of his character, of course, but he has adapted it so that it is a positive help in such an affair as this. You can be sure that he has, so far as it is possible, studied this case from every point of view. He likes to get under the skin of other people, so to speak, to try to understand why they have done what they have done and what they are likely to do in future. It is very difficult to out-guess him. And on this occasion it is easy to forget that he did not know anything about this situation until yesterday at about eleven o'clock in the morning. Under twenty hours, in other words."

"You've got a point there," agreed Wrightson. "Okay, so you can't pull the wool over his eyes, I grant you that. And he hasn't had much chance to shine on this job. Truth is," the little man declared earnestly, "every flicking thing went wrong. Blimey, if I hadn't turned up like a bad penny you and him might've bin on morgue slabs by now. What a turnup for the book that would be."

"And he will find some way of showing his gratitude."

"Aw, forget it," said Wrightson. "I don't want no thanks. Just a way of paying back a little bit of wot Mr.

Ar's done for me and Bill Ebbutt and Gawd knows how many other blokes. Do you know what Lil Ebbutt was telling me? Got a special fund for anyone in trouble, Mr. Ar has. Ebbutt dishes the dough out, calls it donation from Mr. Anonymouse or something. But I expect you knew. What I say is, though," went on Wrightson earnestly, "he's not hisself. I'm not sure that three or four hours sleep will put him right, neither."

"We shall see what we shall see," said Jolly sententiously.

"Blimey, that's original," Wrightson scoffed, and picked up a test tube which Jolly had discarded; and dropped it. "Here that's 'ot. What are you doing, anyway, Mr. Jolly?"

Jolly didn't answer at once, but was watching a curious sediment in the test tube he was holding over the long flame. His lips were set tightly, his eyes were hard. "What—" began Wrightson.

"I have been testing for purity, as Dangerfield was here for nearly half an hour," Jolly said. "There is a substantial quantity of a coarser white powder in this flour. If that is curare, it is quite enough to kill several people."

"Blimey!" breathed Percy Wrightson.

.   .   .   .   .

Rollison did his best to empty his mind of all thought of the affair when he went to bed, soon after Betty Oliver had been persuaded to go into the spare room, and rest for a while. In fact she hadn't taken a lot of persuasion. Almost his last conscious thought had been of the way she had talked about being in love with Alec Dangerfield, and that set his mind on a completely new track; but his head ached and he knew that he could not hope to think logically about it. He had given Jolly instructions to call him in any emergency, or else at one o'clock; but he had an alarm clock by his bedside, because he doubted whether Jolly would wake him, thinking he needed much more sleep. The clock was set for one-fifteen.

He heard the alarm as if a long way off. He knew that it was for him, but he did not want to listen and did not want to stir. He turned over, trying to close his ears to the insistent sound, but it was no use. He stretched out for the clock, in exasperation. His eyes flickered open, and he saw Jolly at the door, carrying a tea tray as if this were a normal morning; that was the first thought he gave to what had happened.

Then he glanced at the clock; it pointed to a quarter past four, not past one. He lay flat on his back, looking at Jolly accusingly, and Jolly placed the tea tray on the bedside table and said:

"Good afternoon, sir. I trust you slept well."

"Well enough for you to sneak in and alter that alarm," Rollison said.

"I am afraid I must admit to that, sir," said Jolly placidly, "but it was largely because of a new situation. I tested the foodstuffs in the larder, and found a sediment, and on analysis by a chemist friend of mine, it proves to be curare." Jolly said all this in an even voice, while Rollison felt increasing alarm. Finally, Jolly said: "In view of the acute danger, sir, I felt it essential that you should be fully rested before you took any further action."

"I see," said Rollison slowly and thoughtfully. "Quite right. Thanks, Jolly. First Percy Wrightson, then you. I should be dead. Why me, Jolly?"

"Don't you know, sir?"

"Not yet," said Rollison, heartily, and he began to sit up. "No other emergencies?"

"None, sir."

"Where is Miss Oliver?"

"She has decided to spend a few days with Mrs. Dangerfield, sir. I have the address, of course. I prepared lunch for them, as Mr. Grice telephoned me to say that Mrs. Dangerfield would be back about half past twelve. They left a little after two-thirty. Ebbutt's men and two men from New Scotland Yard were following them."

"Hmm," mused Rollison. "Ever heard that story about the stable door? What else did Grice say?"

"That the lady's statement appeared to be comprehensive but hardly helpful."

"And?"

"That Claude Dangerfield insists that he did not kil Mr. Oliver. The drug, curare—the same drug as that which killed the man Smith and the woman in Paris, and which I found here—was administered in a whisky and soda which Mr. Oliver had as a night-cap. There appears to be no doubt about that. The call from Paris has been traced—it was from a public call box. Nothing has been found in Paris or at Mitten Mews or Mountain Street which offers any assistance to the police. In fact," went on Jolly, with a note of satisfaction in his voice, "Mr. Grice was honest enough to admit that he is no further on than he was when he left here this morning. Percy Wrightson's word for it is flummoxed."

"Where's Percy?"

"He will be returning at about half past six."

"We mustn't forget that gold medal for him," Rollison remarked. "And for you. How long had you been tied up in my chair?"

"About half an hour, sir. I regret that I was taken completely unawares by the two men when they called. Only Dangerfield was at the door, the other man was by the wall, and—well, sir, I was quickly overpowered. If I had been more cautious—"

"Forget it," said Rollison, and held out his cup for a refill. "No one else dead of curare poisoning, I trust?"

"No so far as we know, sir."

"A quarter past four," remarked Rollison, thoughtfully. "The Dangerfield Art Agency will probably be open until five thirty. I've just time to look round." He pushed back the bedclothes. "I'll wear my light grey suit, and I want to be out of here in half an hour."

"Very well, sir," said Jolly.

In thirty-one minutes, precisely, Rollison was walking along Gresham Terrace, aware that two of Ebbutt's men were following him, and that there was a man from the Yard at either end of the street. He also knew that Jolly and Grice, with Ebbutt's connivance, had arranged this, knew how alarmed Jolly was. Justifiably, too, they believed that he was in grave danger. He agreed with them, but outwardly gave no sign of it. He was freshly shaven and showered, immaculate in the pale grey suit and pale blue socks, tie and breast pocket handkerchief, and he looked almost the dandy as he reached Piccadilly with the phalanx behind him. A taxi was coming from behind him, too, and he let it pass, then recognised the driver as one of Ebbutt's boxing hopes. He grinned and whistled, and the taxi stopped.

"Hullo, Charlie. You ever heard of Forsett Place, near the Strand?"

"Practically born there," Charlie declared. He slammed home his gears, and set the cab hurtling towards Hyde Park Corner, cut across the bows of a bus, and swung into Green Park, past Buckingham Palace and towards Admiralty Arch. Rollison knew that he was making sure that no one could follow them, but the danger was less from anyone behind than from someone who might expect him at the Dangerfield Art Agency.

Whoever was behind this thing might be waiting for him as Claude Dangerfield had waited at the flat.

Rollison kept asking the question which had pre-occupied him most; why try to kill *him*? The obvious answer was because he knew something which was vital, perhaps fatal, to Claude Dangerfield's employers.

What did he know? Was it something that Alec Dangerfield was supposed to have told him?

The taxi sped round Trafalgar Square, blessed with luck at all the traffic lights, and drew up in a side street leading off the Strand. A year ago this had been a narrow, twisting lane leading down to the river with a short flight of steps in the middle, and either side had been rows of old Regency houses, attractive to look at, beloved of architects, hated by sanitary engineers. In its place was a modern office block with pale grey stone outside, vast acres of glass, a wide carriage way, commissionaires in fine plum-coloured uniforms. Rollison went in.

The whole of the ground floor except the hall was obviously given over to one firm, the New World Travel Association. Beyond gleaming and swinging glass doors were large counters and many desks and as many attrac-tive looking girls and well-dressed young men attending to the inquiries and the needs of the customers who were on the other side of counters and desks.

Obviously this was a flourishing business, and yet Rollison had never heard of the New World Travel Association until that morning. In Dangerfield's pocket there had been the empty envelope which had con-tained his air ticket, and he remembered that that envelope had been printed:

New World Travel Association
Luxury Travel At Popular Prices

"Can I help you, sir?" inquired an elevator attendant.

"I'm looking for the Dangerfield Art Agency."

"That is on the seventh and top floor, sir. Elevator Number 4, please," the spruce young man said, and stood aside. Rollison saw one of Grice's men and one of Ebbutt's men enter the building, and was not surprised when without a word to the attendants they joined him in the lift with three other people, all of whom got out at the third floor.

The lift doors opened straight into the general office of the Art Agency, and Rollison got his first surprise. He had always imagined that Alec Dangerfield was in business in quite a small way, more as a rich man's plaything. This gave a very different impression. On the walls were paintings, all of them originals of book covers, some extremely well-known on the bookstalls. Glass walls carried the legends: *Art—Editorial. Accounts. Art—Commercial, Television*, and on other doors were names already familiar to Rollison—*Mr. Alec Dangerfield, Mr. Marvin Oliver, Betty Oliver*. This place was both plush and lush, and the specimens of artwork round the walls were of very high quality.

A well-groomed, well-dressed young woman of no special beauty approached him from the other side of the counter. Two others went to the counter to attend to the Yard man and Ebbutt's man. Among the clerks working on the other side of the counter, in a kind of general office, were at least two of Grice's plain clothes officers; there could hardly be danger here.

"Can I help you, sir?" the girl asked.

"Is Mrs. Dangerfield in?" inquired Rollison.

"No, sir, she hasn't been in today."

"Is Miss Betty Oliver in?"

"Yes, sir," the girl answered unexpectedly. "She is

very busy with personal matters but if you will give me your name I'm sure she will see you if she possibly can."

"Thank you," said Rollison. He gave his card, saw the girl glance down at it, and start, saw the way she looked at him as she went to Betty Oliver's door. He felt a curious edginess which was not usual, and also a flatness as of disappointment. It would be far more difficult to obtain a picture of the situation here than he had hoped; a small office with a staff of two or three would have been much more promising.

The girl came hurrying back.

"I'm very sorry, Mr. Rollison," she said, "but Miss Oliver says that she cannot possibly spare you even five minutes. She has just time to sign some letters and then to keep a personal appointment. You—you may know that Mr. Marvin Oliver, her brother—"

"Yes, I know," said Rollison, and smiled, and lifted a flap in the smooth topped desk and went towards Betty Oliver's door. He meant to find out why she had refused to see him.

18

FEAR

ROLLISON pushed open the door of Betty Oliver's office. She was standing up at her desk, collecting some papers, and jerked her head up. Her eyes looked enormous and glittering bright, as with fear. Of him? In a corner behind her was another door, and she glanced at that desperately, as if she were longing to rush out through it. He allowed his door to close, aware that the tall girl from the reception desk was just outside.

"Hallo, Betty," Rollison said, quietly. "What's the hurry?"

"I—I have to go and look after things," Betty answered agitatedly. "I—I only came in for an hour to sign one or two letters and look after desperately urgent work. It—it has to go on, the whole business has to go on, and with Alec away everything was left to me and Marvin. It—it was my duty to come."

"I see," said Rollison.

On the desk was a brief case, wide open; it was obvious that she had been going to push the papers inside it. Rollison showed no immediate interest in the papers but went nearer the desk. The door opened behind him, and the tall girl asked:

"Is everything all right, Miss Oliver?"

"Yes, yes, it's all right, Mr. Rollison had to see me, I can understand that now. You—you needn't wait, Jane."

"Well, if you're sure." The girl sounded dubious.

"Don't stand there arguing, get out and close the door!" Betty screeched at her.

The girl stalked out; the door nearly slammed. Betty lowered herself into a comfortable looking swivel chair, and covered her face in her hands. Rollison still did not take any overt notice of the papers she had collected, but he glanced at the open door. He heard a stealthy movement, and he passed the desk swiftly, stood by the wall alongside the door, and waited. Then he saw one of Grice's men, obviously outside to make sure that Betty Oliver didn't acquire the killing habit. Rollison revealed himself, winked, and went back to Betty. She was pushing the papers into the brief-case now, sniffing back tears.

"Betty, who told you not to see me?" asked Rollison.

"That—that's not true! I just don't feel I can talk about it any more."

"Who told you?"

"It's not true, I tell you. Don't stand there calling me a liar!"

"You're a liar, Betty, and you're lying to help the man who murdered your brother."

"You—you—you *swine*!" she cried, and struck out at him. He half expected the attack, ducked, then caught her wrists and held her hands tightly with one hand, leaving the other free. For a moment she writhed and struggled, gasping for breath, showing her teeth, glaring; then she seemed to collapse, but Rollison did not let her go. He drew her to one side, picked up the brief-case with his free hand, and shook all the papers out. Betty stared at them, the glitter in her eyes suddenly dulled.

These were mostly folders, used as files, and the first was marked: *Smith, Gabriel*, the second *Shawn, Simon R.*, and the next *Benoit, A*. There were other files which slid out of the brief-case, all marked with a name—and all of them names which Claude Dangerfield had given him.

"So you were taking the evidence away," said Rollison. "Who for, Betty?"

"I was just taking home some papers to work on. I can't work here tonight, I simply can't."

"Who made you do it? And who told you not to say anything else to me. Was it Katherine?"

"*No!*"

"Who was it? Why did you come here at all? You didn't say anything about coming. I understood from Jolly that you were going to stay with Katherine for a few days, and you certainly didn't look like working then. Why don't you tell the truth? A lot of people have died because of what's happening here. Who told you——?"

Unthinkingly, and because she seemed to have given up the physical struggle, Rollison slackened his grip. Suddenly she pulled herself free, tried to grab the brief-case, and rushed towards the door. Instead of keeping the brief-case upright, she spilled all the files over the floor. Every paper fell loose and fluttered about, some into the corners, some out of the open doorway at the back of the office. When she realised what had happened, she stopped moving, and stared wildly down at the papers, pressing her hands against her forehead as if her head were about to split.

"Who was it?" Rollison asked, and added very quietly: "Was it Alec?"

"No!" she gasped. "No, it wasn't, it wasn't Alec! I haven't heard from Alec! He's been missing for seven weeks, what kind of a fool *are* you? You know he's been missing, you've been looking for him. You're absolutely useless, you've done more harm than good."

"Was it Alec Dangerfield?" insisted Rollison.

She closed her eyes, and for a moment he thought that

she was going to collapse, and in his mind he was carried back to the moment when Katherine Dangerfield had collapsed in Paris, after realising that Shawn had been murdered.

"Betty, I needn't tell the police yet," Rollison said, "and I won't tell them unless I'm sure they ought to know in order to save life. Was it Alec?"

She didn't look at him, but muttered: "Yes."

"Just what happened?"

"He—he telephoned me," she muttered. "It was such a shock, I was so afraid he was dead, and I didn't really expect to hear from him again. He—he asked me to get all these files out, and to take them away from the office before you or the police came for them, and—and I had to do it." For the first time she looked at him, but there was a guilty air about her, as if she realised that she had been taking part in some crime. "I had to do what Alec asked me. I told you before. I love him so."

"Even if he's a murderer?"

"I can't help what he is. I've got to help him, he's all I care about."

"Is he?" asked Rollison, softly. "I wonder. Where were you to deliver the papers?"

"I—I was just to put them in a brief-case and—and give them to a man I would meet on the ground floor."

"When?"

"Alec—Alec said the man would be waiting from five o'clock onwards."

"Right," said Rollison. "You'll do just that. You can take the brief-case down in the lift, and two men will be with you—a Scotland Yard officer and a friend of mine. If you give the man who takes the case the slightest hint that anything's wrong, both you and the man will be taken to the Yard for questioning. Is that clear?"

"Yes," Betty said, and more life crept into her voice, although her eyes were still dull and lack-lustre. "Why don't you let me go? Why don't you let me help Alec?"

"You know why you can't," Rollison said.

"If you hadn't come, no one could have stopped me!"

"But I did come," Rollison pointed out. "Officer," he called, and on the instant the Scotland Yard man appeared. "Get Bill Ebbutt's chap, and then come in and help pick up these papers, will you?" Rollison said. "I can brief you afterwards."

"Right away, sir."

"Thanks," said Rollison.

Betty Oliver went down on her knees and began to fumble for the papers, and he saw that in spite of her tension and the situation she put the right ones in the proper folders; she was automatically efficient as a secretary. In a minute the two men came to help. Rollison looked at his watch and saw that it was nearly half past five. He wondered fleetingly what would have happened if Jolly had let him sleep for another hour, but that wasn't important: at last he was getting some kind of a break. He waited until the papers were all in proper order, then briefed the two men, who went with Betty Oliver to the lift. She didn't look round at him, but stared at the floor, as if all her spirit had gone.

Rollison went into the general office. If he showed himself downstairs it might warn the man who was to come for the brief-case, so he must stay here for five minutes at least.

Most of the staff had already left. The tall receptionist was standing with her small hat on, umbrella in hand, obviously not sure what to do. A middle-aged man was standing by her. They looked at Betty Oliver, at the lift, then at Rollison, as if they could not make up their minds what they should do. Another of Grice's men was by the door leading to the staircase, so that he could check everyone who came in and out, either by the stairs or by the lifts.

Rollison asked the middle-aged man: "Do you know where Mr. Alec Dangerfield is?"

"No, Mr. Rollison, I don't," the man answered hurriedly. "I understood that he had gone to America, but I must say I was puzzled because there were none of the usual cables and urgent letters. Usually when he goes abroad we're kept extremely busy. I am Joseph Pengelly, the secretary accountant here, in charge of the financial side of the business. I am supposed to be informed of everything that's going on," he added with injured dignity, "but now that Miss Oliver tells me that Mr. Dangerfield is missing—well, that is a complete surprise. It's appalling. Appalling!"

"Have there been any messages from him?"

"Not as far as I *know*."

"Would the operator at the switchboard recognise his voice?"

"Yes," interpolated the girl named Jane. She was very well made up, nicely dressed, nicely shaped, with long slim legs. "I was on the exchange all the afternoon until just before you came, Mr. Rollison."

"Did Mr. Alec Dangerfield telephone Miss Oliver?"

"No, she had no telephone calls. I am quite sure."

"Did she have any visitors?"

"No."

"Thanks," said Rollison. "Sorry I've troubled you." He turned towards the lifts, trying not to dwell on the developments downstairs, but not knowing what had happened was almost unbearable. It would be over now.

He went towards a lift, which according to the indicator

was stationary on the fourth floor. It began to move directly he pressed the call button. He stepped in, and the girl and the middle-aged man followed him, one fussily, one diffidently. He wondered if Betty Oliver had really gone back to Katherine's flat, as she had told Jolly—if she had, she had probably received her instructions there. The police as well as Ebbutt's man had been following her; they would know.

The lift seemed to crawl, much more slowly than the one the boy had operated in the George V Hotel. Even the automatically controlled gates seemed to take an age to open. The moment they did they opened on to disaster.

Betty Oliver was stretched out on the floor by the wall, and a man was bending over her. Another man was swearing. An alarmed looking crowd of people were between the doors leading from the New World Travel Association and the street. Outside, three policemen were holding everyone back. The shouting man was a stranger to Rollison. He was held in a tight grip by Grice's man, and in his left hand was Betty's brief-case.

Rollison was looking beyond him into the big central office of the travel agency, where only a few people were gathered, most of them near the door and staring through the thick glass.

"Had quite a job, sir," the Yard man said. "He took the case, and we gave him a couple of yards start to see where he was going, hoping to follow him as you said, sir. Then he tried to get into the Travel Agency. There are three or four ways out of there, so I decided to stop him. Put up a hell of a fight."

"Yes," said Rollison. "What happened to Miss Oliver?"

"Just fainted I think, sir," the man said, and then a glint of alarm showed in his eyes, and he gasped: "My

God!" On that instant his grip must have slackened, and the man with the brief-case jerked himself free and rushed towards the door. For a moment, only Rollison was in his way. He looked as if he would like to kill Rollison, who simply stepped to one side and stretched out his leg. The man tripped. Rollison watched him as he thudded down, and let him begin to struggle up, and then hit him savagely on the side of the jaw. A woman cried: "*Oh!*"

Rollison rubbed his knuckles, and said with quiet urgency: "Get Miss Oliver across to Charing Cross Hospital, and have her treated as having taken a curare drug orally. It's vitally urgent—she could be dead within the hour." He turned towards the man he had knocked down again, and asked in the same hard voice: "Where were you going to take the brief-case?" The man was too dazed to answer, perhaps too dazed even to understand, but Rollison gripped his arm and shouted the question. At the same time he kept a covert watch on the crowd between him and the doors of the New World Travel Association. He saw no one who he recognised, but saw one man with his right hand in his coat pocket; it bulged as if he had a weapon hidden. Two or three people were close to this man, who was edging his way forward to the front of the crowd. Rollison saw that something poked out against his pocket.

"*Tell me who you were working for!*" Rollison shouted, and then gripped the man's arm, twisted, and sent him slithering along the imitation marble floor. A woman cried out again, there was a sharp report of a shot, a crack of sound as a bullet struck the hard floor just where the arrested man had been.

Rollison leapt towards the man who had fired through his pocket, and who was now pointing the gun at him.

went on softly: "They're as ruthless and cold-blooded a mob as I've met in all the years I've been at this game. They've killed mercilessly to make sure they can't be traced. They must have realised that if ever I began to realise what was happening I'd tell you—and they wanted to make sure that I couldn't. They also wanted to make sure that when you started digging, all the evidence would be destroyed. I think they had a kind of blue print for action the moment the situation became dangerous."

"And you made the crack widen too quickly," Grice said.

"Never felt so much as if I were punching at a pillow," said Rollison. "And when I heard that Marvin Oliver has died—" he paused. "Any news from the hospital about his sister, I wonder?"

"If there were, we'd have heard," said Grice. "Did you suggest she might try to poison herself?"

"I don't even know that she did," said Rollison. "She may not have realised that she was taking poison. We've a lot to find out about Betty. She was obviously under some kind of pressure, and did what she was told. She was given orders about the files, she was told who to give them to, and took or was also given poison to try to make sure that she could never talk freely to us. She named Alec Dangerfield—saying that he telephoned her—but you can't yet transmit drugs by telephone. Can you?"

"You can transmit smells from the screen," Grice said, almost absently. "Let's get across to the hospital and see if she can talk."

"That's if she's alive," Rollison said glumly.

.   .   .   .   .

Betty Oliver was in a coma after taking a substantial dose of morphine, not of curare; not all of the narcotic drug had been absorbed into the system. Judging from the amount found only partly digested in the stomach contents, the doctors guessed that it had been taken about two hours before the time of her collapse. They were hopeful that they could bring her round, but not certain.

"How long will it be before she can talk?" asked Grice.

"I should say at least twenty-four hours, and possibly much longer—say twenty-four hours from the time she comes round, provided she comes round," the doctor answered.

"Thank you," said Grice, bleakly.

It was nearly nine o'clock when he left the hospital with Rollison. A police car was waiting outside for him, and he stepped inside and immediately flicked on the radio and asked for the Information Room. When it answered, he asked:

"Anything from Morrison?"

"He won't say a word, sir."

"What about his fellow directors?"

"There was only Mr. Alec Dangerfield, sir." Rollison could just make out the words.

"Right," said Grice. He rang off and looked at Rollison grimly. "This is one occasion when I wish you'd had Morrison on your own for an hour, you might have got something from him. It begins to look as if Alec Dangerfield discovered the racket, and they put him away to make sure he couldn't break it up. Is that what you're thinking?"

"I'm wondering why his brother called him a righteous humbug," Rollison said, "and I'm wondering whether that was a kind of cover for Alec. If Claude knew his number was up, he might have wanted to try to save his brother. Sneering and swearing about him would go a long way towards making it look as if Alec knew nothing about it. But we have Betty Oliver's statement about receiving a telephone message from Alec. One thing is pretty certain," Rollison went on thoughtfully, "Betty would lie for Alec, and I fancy she would even die for him. She just didn't have the strength of will to keep his name back, and she's got guts all right, or—"

"Or what?" Grice demanded.

"Or for some reason she gave Alec's name to keep someone else in the clear."

"Who—" Grice began, only to stop abruptly. He looked at Rollison in the small confines of the car, and asked: "Have you any idea?"

"No, but I may know someone who has," Rollison said dryly. "Bill, my next call will be on Katherine Danger-field, who hated my guts this morning because I'd brought you into the case. That could have been because she thought I'd be ready to hush up certain facts, but the police couldn't. I've a feeling that Katherine Dangerfield has been keeping a lot back."

"It wouldn't surprise me," Grice said. "Well, I've had two policewomen and a man at her flat. All the foodstuffs have been checked—after the discovery of curare in your larder I wasn't taking any chances. No one can get at the woman."

Rollison didn't answer.

"I put her through a pretty tough interview earlier, and she showed up very well," Grice went on.

"Yes, she shows up well," Rollison agreed. "Thanks, Bill. I'll talk to the lady. In fact I think I'll telephone her and tell her that I'll be round to see her at half past ten or so, and we'll see if she sits in and waits for me, or whether she does a Betty Oliver and tries to back out of an interview. Will you drop me at home, first? I'll telephone from there."

"Yes, of course," Grice said. "I can tell you one or two

other things. Betty Oliver had nothing to drink at her office—there was no cup or glass on her desk and she didn't go into the washroom."

"Thanks," said Rollison. "That could help."

Ten minutes later Grice dropped Rollison outside the flat in Gresham Terrace, where a Yard man and one of Ebbutt's "boys" were on duty. Rollison acknowledged both as he went in, called good night to Grice, then hurried upstairs. He was hungry and he was anxious— and when he reached the top landing and the door opened, he realised that Jolly had a certain anxiety, too.

"Everything all right, Jolly? I'm famished, and—"

"Dinner can be served at any time, sir," said Jolly, "but I thought that you would like to wait until—"

He broke off, as Katherine Dangerfield appeared in the doorway of the big room.

20

DINNER

"Hallo, Rolly," she greeted quietly.

"Not Mr. Rollison any more?" said Rollison.

"I think I did you an injustice this morning," Katherine said.

"You'll be doing me a worse one if you're not hungry," Rollison replied. "Have you had dinner?"

"No. I would be glad to dine with you."

"Fine. Fix it fast, Jolly." Rollison was probably a little too breezy, but that was quite deliberate. He took Katherine's hand as they went into the room, where the first thing he noticed was that the hangman's rope was back in position. The second, now that the light was better, was that Katherine was quite at her loveliest. It occurred to him that she looked more like a painting by one of the artists whose work was on the walls of the Dangerfield Agency than like a real person; and that was a point to remember. Her matter-of-factness in all the circumstances had a touch of unreality, too.

Was she a little unreal, as a person?

Or was she acting a part?

"What will you have to drink?" he asked. "I need a stiff one."

"Dubonnet, please," she said, and like Percy Wrightson, Rollison thought of the word subdued. He poured out, a stiff whisky and soda for himself, they touched glasses, and he sipped his drink. "Ah, that is really good!

Just another tot? I must really go and get some of the printing ink off my fingers." He turned his back on her, pushed his nearly full glass behind some books, and half-filled another.

"Printing ink?" Katherine inquired more keenly.

"Yes," said Rollison and looked at her steadily. "We've found where they print the notes, how they distribute them, where they keep them."

Her eyes seemed to light up.

"Have you found Alec?"

"Not yet."

"Rolly," she said, and came nearer to him, her cool fingers touching the back of his hand lightly, "don't ever lose sight of the fact that Alec is the most important thing, will you?"

"For you he may be," said Rollison. "I'll remember." He put down his glass, said: "Make yourself at home, Katherine," and went out. Jolly was putting the finishing touches to a casserole, the standby dish whenever it was uncertain what time Rollison would be home. "Get the whisky glass from behind the books when we start dinner, and test it for curare, or for morphine," Rollison whispered.

"Very good, sir."

"How long will we be, Jolly?" Rollison asked in a louder voice.

"No more than five minutes, sir."

"Fine!" Rollison said, and whistled when he went into his bathroom. He washed at leisure, and it was over five minutes before he got back to the big room, where Katherine was studying the Trophy Wall with an interest which seemed to include every one. As he came in and went straight to his drink, she looked at him; nothing suggested that she was watching whether he drank or not. He pretended to sip.

"Bizarre, aren't they?" he said.

"What will be your souvenir of this case?" Katherine asked. "A lock of hair, like that? A poison tablet, like that? A bullet?" She pointed to different articles as she spoke, and each time she looked round Rollison had the glass at his lips. It was a peculiar feeling that the drink might be poisoned; that he might die if he drank it. "Or a silk stocking like that?" She touched a nylon stocking which had a daub of red nail varnish on it.

"Certainly not," said Rollison. "I should ask the Powers That Be for a specimen of each of the forged bank-notes, and Jolly would make a frame for me—like they do in the windows of the *bureaux de change* on the continent."

"You could have one of Alec's favourite paintings by the Agency artists," Katherine pointed out.

"Yes, I suppose so," agreed Rollison, "but—" He broke off when Jolly appeared, and murmured that dinner was served, took Katherine's arm and led her to the small alcove at the far end of the room. Jolly served cold salmon for the first course, and there was a slender bottle of *Liebfraumilch* on the table, the cork drawn. They were half-way through the salmon and Katherine was eating with obvious relish when Rollison asked:

"Why did you come tonight? And why the change of mood?"

"I had to see you," she said. "I had to talk to you. I know I was unforgivable this morning, but I was so bitterly disappointed. I think I hated you when I found you here with that policeman."

"Why?"

"Don't pretend not to understand," she said. "You knew what they threatened to do to Alec if I sent for the police."

"Ah," said Rollison, and forked a piece of salmon.
"Katherine, it isn't possible to go around dodging corpses,
being suspected of murder, having the French police
chasing you out of the country and the English police
waiting to welcome you in, without making some kind of
explanation."

"I realise that now," she said, "but when we came to
your flat, and the police were already there and obviously
knew everything—" She broke off. "That's why I was so
beastly."

"The only reason?"

"Yes."

"Katherine."

"Yes?"

"Why did you poison Marvin Oliver?"

Rollison popped the salmon into his mouth and ate it
with evident relish, watching the woman all the time. She
stiffened. Her hands moved, just a little, and the fork
made a slight chink of sound against her plate; that was
all. She looked at him without speaking, and he took
another piece of salmon, with almost impudent deliberation, and waited for her. Jolly hovered in the doorway,
then disappeared.

"Do you really think I did?" she asked at last. "Or
was that a trick question?"

"It was a straight question."

"Why do you ask it?"

"You could have gone to see Marvin Oliver last night,
you were out of the Marigold Club for at least an hour—
my men told me that. They also told me that you were
lost near Mountain Street." He let that sink in. "And
you were with Betty all the afternoon until she left for
the Agency office. Neither she nor her brother would
suspect you would poison him."

"No, they wouldn't, would they?" Katherine asked in a choky voice, and then as if to show him that she had complete control of her nerves, she took a piece of salmon, ate it, and said with quiet vehemence: "No, I didn't poison Marvin, and I don't know who did!"

"Did anyone come to see Betty this afternoon?"

"No."

"Did she have a telephone call?"

"Yes."

"Did she say who from?"

"She said it was from Mr. Pengelly, the Secretary Accountant of the Agency, who draws all the cheques. He told her that several cheques had to be signed, and Betty can sign up to fifty pounds. That's why she went to the office today—isn't it?"

"Is it what she told you?"

"Yes."

"Apparently it wasn't the reason. Did you know that she was in love with your husband?"

Katherine caught her breath, and her fingers stiffened again, but it was more with surprise than with shock, and after a moment she answered:

"Yes."

"Was there an *affaire*?"

"No."

"Can you be sure?"

"I think so," Katherine said. "I think I know Alec as well as it's possible to know a man, and I don't believe he would carry on a clandestine love affair with anyone, least of all Betty Oliver. And if he were doing anything like that I don't think he could hide it from me. He is the most transparently honest man I've ever known."

"Or you think he is."

"Are you saying that he is in any way implicated in

these crimes?" asked Katherine, and there was heat in her voice as she went on: "Because if you are, I think it's a complete waste of time even talking about it."

"Either he's involved," said Rollison, "or Betty Oliver lied to me when she said he telephoned her and told her to get certain files from the Agency."

"Betty says that Alec—" This time he appeared to have sparked her to astonishment. She pushed her plate back, and said in a hopeless kind of voice: "Really, this is carrying everything to a point of absurdity. I don't for a moment believe that Alec talked to Betty. Apart from anything else, I don't think she could have kept it from me. Certainly she would have shown some kind of excitement when she heard his voice."

"Unless she was expecting to hear it."

"No," said Katherine, vehemently. "I don't believe this for a moment. Betty was lying if she really told you that Alec telephoned her."

"That's what she told me."

"Then why—" Katherine began, and broke off. She picked up her wine glass, sipped, looked at him over the edge, and went on: "Why don't you talk to Betty? I can't believe she would ever be able to withstand your questioning."

"I can't talk to her."

"Why not?"

"Guess," invited Rollison.

For a moment Katherine looked puzzled; then understanding seemed to dawn in her eyes, as if she were both astounded and alarmed. She leaned across the table, hands raised a little, and the glitter in her eyes gave her an additional touch of beauty; yet there was still a suggestion that it was affectation.

"She hasn't been—*murdered!*" When Rollison didn't

respond, she went on huskily: "She can't have been. Not while you and the police were looking after her, not while—"

"She's unconscious," Rollison interrupted. "She might be saved. As far as we know, you are the only person she saw after she left this flat this afternoon, until she reached her office a little after half past four. The police have checked. She had nothing to eat or drink at the office. There was no cup on her desk, no glass of water. The time that the drug takes to be effective varies but the probability is that she took it about half past three to four o'clock this afternoon, when she was with you."

Katherine said: "So that's why you think I poisoned Marvin. Rolly, I—" She broke off, and looked towards the Trophy Wall; it was easy to believe that her eyes were misted with tears. "Is this what the police think, too?" she asked at last.

"It's a possibility they're considering."

"Why didn't they come to arrest me?"

"I arranged with Grice to talk to you first." Rollison glanced up and nodded to Jolly, who came in at once and removed their plates.

"All I can say is that I didn't give Betty poison, and I didn't poison Marvin. I went to my own flat last night, I had to get some clothes and oddments. I told Miss Stephenson. I can't help it if the police lost me, I simply walked to my flat and back. Berkeley Square is quite close to Mountain Street, as you probably know."

"Yes, I know," agreed Rollison. "Do you know Mr. Morrison of the New World Travel Association?"

"I've met him," said Katherine.

"How and when?"

"He wanted some posters and some brochures done, and we specialise in that kind of work," answered Katherine.

"He telephoned Alec a few months ago. He came round for a drink one evening, as they couldn't fit in a convenient time for an appointment at the office."

"Did anything come of the interest?"

"I don't think so."

"Why not?"

"Good heavens, how do you expect me to know that?" Katherine flushed. At the same moment Jolly came in with the duck, placed the dish in front of Rollison, and made magic with plates and dishes which stood on a hot plate at one side. "There are dozens of inquiries which lead to nothing, and Alec wouldn't worry about telling me about business which didn't come off."

"I see," said Rollison. He served the duck, which had a remarkably appetising odour, allowed Jolly to offer the *petit pois*, tiny new potatoes and a cauliflower au gratin. Then Jolly went to the door, turned to face Rollison, and shook his head.

So there was no poison in that whisky.

Rollison began to eat, without answering Katherine. After an angry pause she began to eat too, with a surprisingly hearty appetite. When she had nearly finished, Rollison looked across at her, smiled, and asked:

"Kate, where's Alec?"

21

FALSE EVIDENCE

"So you don't believe me," Katherine said in a low-pitched voice. "You don't believe or trust me at all, do you?"

"No," said Rollison.

"If I knew where Alec was, why should I have come to you for help?"

"But you didn't come to me for help," Rollison told her. "You knew that I was after Benoit, and had to find out why, so you pretended he was frightening you. So as to make your story seem plausible, he was always following you about. Quite clever, Kate, but not clever enough. When I thought about it, so much of your story didn't stand up. You haunted restaurants and cafés for me, you claimed—but didn't try the best hotels. So, you knew where I was."

Katherine made no comment.

"You and Claude went all to pieces after the Benoit incident," said Rollison. "Or was Claude away from Paris, and did he leave too much to you?" He paused again, and then went on: "I think Claude gave the orders but daren't stay in Paris to make sure they were properly carried out. Let's see what happened. Once I'd put Benoit away I was to be killed, and Shawn was sent to kill me. And to kill you, Kate—by that time Claude was showing that he was frightened of everyone, including you. When that piece of masonry was loosened it was Claude's way of saying goodbye to you. Wasn't it?"

She kept quite still and silent.

"But you tried to keep the blood off your hands," Rollison told her, still very softly. "You had plenty of opportunity to kill me, but you wouldn't kill anyone. Claude knew you couldn't be trusted to kill, especially when he had Shawn killed in such a way that you could be blamed for it. After the failure to crush us to death he had us both watched, and he tried to finish me off with two men and a taxi driver—I shouldn't have taken the first available cab, should I?"

Katherine might have been made of stone for all the movement she made.

"You must have been feeling pretty grim," went on the Toff, "for after Shawn, Gabby Smith and his sweetie went out like a light. Claude knew that all who worked for him would do exactly as they were told—except sweet Kate, of course!—and he told Smith and Madame Blanc to kill Shawn, and to move the body, and then to go back to the hotel for their clothes—knowing that he was going to murder them as soon as they got back to their *appartement*. What a stew you must have been in when you knew what had happened to them, Kate.

"Because soon it would be a fight between the two of you—between you and Claude. He wasn't at all happy about what you might have told me after the masonry trick, that's why he kept me on a piece of string at my flat —he could have killed me, but there was something he wanted desperately to know, and it seemed obvious to me that he could learn it only from you. In fact after he tried to kill us together, and after he framed you for Shawn's murder, I think you made him realise that you still had an ace. That's why he left you alive, after all.

That's why he kept on questioning me, wanting to find out what you'd told me."

"I think you must be mad," Katherine said, in a clear voice.

"Oh, no, not me. Claude perhaps; certainly he was nearly mad to give Shawn the killing job. He should have known that the odds in a tussle between me and Shawn were all in my favour, and that once I got the best of Shawn I would be right on the ball.

"Yes, Shawn was a mistake, but Claude made plenty—most of them forced on him by one uncertain factor, the one thing he didn't know. The mechanics of the plot were easy. The Agency was an ideal distribution centre for enormous sums in foreign currency, but it was also one which would be closed up immediately suspicion was aroused. So Claude had it all fixed. Everyone was to be killed off once they ran right into trouble, I expect Morrison would have gone sooner or later, but—there was the one thing Claude didn't know, but you did.

"What was it, Kate?

"Where Alec was? Was that Claude's problem? Was he afraid that you and Alec were working together against him? Was he afraid that Alec was still alive?"

Now, his voice was cold and bleak, and he was staring at her coldly.

"None of this is true," Katherine said in a stronger voice.

"Every word of it's true," Rollison asserted. "Let's go through it, item by item. I'm not sure of Alec's position, but I think he is a victim. I should think he discovered what was happening at the vaults at the New World Travel Association, and wanted to stop it. Probably because his brother was deeply involved, and because he didn't know how far it went or how much money was involved, he thought that he could stop it, and hush it up. I can imagine the scene between him and his brother. I can imagine how he confided in you afterwards, not knowing that you were in it up to your neck."

"You are utterly, hopelessly wrong," Katherine declared.

"I don't think so," said Rollison. "I don't know when you realised I was after Benoit, but when you and Claude Dangerfield realised that I was probably investigating the forgeries, you began to follow me, and had your story carefully prepared."

"You are utterly, hopelessly wrong," Katherine said again, but this time her lips were set tightly, and the words seemed to come viciously.

"No, Kate, I'm not," said Rollison. "I've told you— once I had Benoit put away, on a trumped-up charge, I was on the spot. So as to make you look innocent, a tape recorder was put in my room—as if the crooks were determined to find out if I talked to you by telephone, or in person. It was done in haste, and clumsily. Benoit's arrest really caused panic, didn't it?"

Katherine didn't answer.

"As a matter of fact, you did a very convincing job," declared Rollison. "You nearly passed out when Shawn was found dead, and you didn't give me a hint of the truth. You fought hard against it, but couldn't save yourself, although tough and matter-of-fact. The woman I talked to before dinner wasn't likely to pass out at the sight of a dead man—especially a dead man who looked as if he were sleeping. A woman as worried as you were supposed to be wouldn't have eaten with your hearty appetite that day. A woman who had slept as little as you said couldn't have looked as you did—lack of sleep always shows in the eyes. Didn't anyone warn you against the consequences of the simpler lies? You weren't worried about Alec at all, but you were shaken to the core by Shawn's murder because you knew Claude could frame you for it."

"This—this is monstrous," Katherine said in a strangled voice.

"Yes. Monstrous is the word. But you fought back, and even worked with Claude again. I think it's certain that you poisoned Marvin Oliver last night," Rollison went on, "and I'd put a lot of money on you as Betty's poisoner —you slipped her something, probably pretending they were aspirins. You used morphia because a curare death would have made it almost sure she had been murdered— morphia had the required suicide implication. You didn't want her dead too quickly, either. You told her to go and get those files, because they had to be destroyed at once. You told her to tell the police or me that she had had a telephone call from Alec, if she were found out. She obeyed you for one reason only—that's the second reason for my belief that Alec's alive."

Katherine moistened her lips. "Go on," she said. "You're so very clever."

"Betty would lie for Alec, she would even die for him, but she is basically an honest person," Rollison went on. "She might be frightened for herself, but her greatest fear, almost the *raison d'être* of her existence, was love for Alec. So, you told her that he was alive, and that if she did as you instructed he would come through all right. And I think she would want some kind of proof that he was alive, so—where is he, Kate?"

She said: "There isn't a word of truth or sense in what you're saying."

"There is, you know," insisted Rollison. "I may have got some of the motives wrong, but the general principles are about right. You, Claude Dangerfield, Marvin Oliver, and Morrison of New World were the prime movers and, of course, you employed a great number of people who were getting a cut out of the profits—including the cashiers at the Travel Association. The artists were always a danger, too, probably because they had been in it from the beginning, that's one reason why they all had to be killed. Remember how angry you were when you heard what I'd done to Benoit? It really pointed to you as a suspect, as far back as that. The peculiar thing about a case like this," went on Rollison almost dreamily, "is how everything fits into place and makes sense when you know the key to it all."

"I was and am utterly indifferent to Benoit," Katherine declared. "He was known to my husband, not to me. I can't answer for Claude, I am *not* my brother-in-law's keeper, and I can't answer for this Morrison person. I told you the truth from the beginning. My husband disappeared, and I am desperately anxious to find him. As for Shawn—"she gave a high pitched laugh. "I'd never seen a dead man before, and was terribly shocked."

"I daresay—you hadn't bargained for murder at that stage," Rollison said. "But it's all beside the point. Where's Alec, Kate," he insisted. "At your flat? Is there a loft—you're on the top floor, aren't you? I imagine he must be. I imagine that Betty wouldn't have behaved as she did unless she'd actually seen him alive."

Katherine said: "I think it is time I left." She stood up. "I am quite prepared to answer any questions which the police care to put, but I am not prepared to stay here and be insulted any longer."

Rollison smiled broadly.

"Not so good, Kate, not at all in character," he said. "I can understand that you're frightened. I can even understand you thinking that while I can guess at all these things, I can't prove them." She moved across the room to get her handbag. "But you made one fatal mistake by coming here."

"I have done and said nothing to affect the situation by coming here, except to endure an intolerable evening," she retorted coldly.

"Not bad," said Rollison. "Not bad at all. You're trying to make sure that if I've a tape recorder tucked away, not a word you say would betray the part you've played. I've always admired that self-control of yours. In fact as a person I've always been interested in you. There aren't many women—or men for that matter—who can keep their heads as well as you in all kinds of emergency. If you hadn't gone into the forgery business you would have made a very successful businesswoman, Kate. I imagine that Alec wouldn't let you do anything much in the business, that you were bored—"

He was talking to her back. She turned away and picked up her handbag from the arm of her chair. For a moment she stood still, as if to prevent him from seeing her face. He stood up.

"It's important to you because if he's alive, he's your only chance," he said. "You haven't much of a chance as it is, for the police will catch up with you, but I'm the only one who can actually prove a serious crime against you. I'll keep that proof to myself if you'll take me to Alec, and if he's alive. I can't speak for what he'll do."

She turned to face him, and there was no colour at all in her cheeks.

"You have no evidence of any kind against me."

"Oh, yes, I have," said Rollison. "I left you in this room for five minutes this evening, alone. In the five minutes you put curare into my whisky, and had I drunk it, I would have died. You thought it an even chance, because you knew Claude was going to leave curare in foodstuffs here, and probably in my whisky, and it could be assumed that he'd poisoned me. Certainly you would have a good defence if it came to a trial."

She took a step towards him.

"That's a lie, an utter lie! I didn't touch your glass! There couldn't have been poison in it."

"Yes, there could," said Rollison, and called "Jolly". They waited until Jolly appeared, and Rollison asked quietly: "Isn't it true that I instructed you to analyse the whisky in my glass after I had left Mrs. Dangerfield alone?"

"It is, sir."

"What did you find?"

"Substantial quantities of the curare poison, sir, quite sufficient to have proved fatal had you drink the whisky."

"You're both lying," Katherine said hoarsely, but she looked desperately at Jolly now, as if she realised that this lie might be the one thing which could trap her.

"I can further swear in court that I saw Mrs. Dangerfield take a small tablet from her handbag, and drop it into your glass, sir," said Jolly, entering fully into the spirit of this diversion.

"Why you—" Katherine began, but her voice was breaking.

"How about it, Kate?" asked Rollison. "Jolly and I won't tell the police about this provided you take us to Alec. That will give you a fighting chance. If Alec doesn't know you're involved, so much the better."

She closed her eyes.

Rollison was quite sure that he had found the truth, but not sure whether she would give him the information he wanted, not sure whether Alec Dangerfield was alive or dead.

22

ALEC

Rollison felt an almost desperate anxiety for the man whom he had never seen.

If his threat failed, he would have to decide whether to submit false evidence to the police so that they could work on the case knowing they could convict Katherine on a major charge. If it were "proved" that she had administered poison to one person, it would increase the probability that she had administered it to others.

Would Katherine believe that he would carry out his threat?

If she did, she might tell him the truth about her husband and so give herself a slender chance, but even that depended on how much her husband knew—if he were alive.

At heart, Rollison knew and Jolly knew that they could never frame her, could never swear to Grice or to the court that she had tried to poison Rollison. It was simply a question of whether Katherine's nerve were strong enough to withstand the new pressure. From the beginning her nerve had been as strong as the situation called for.

She stood there, tall and beautiful, slender and erect, with her eyes closed. Jolly watched from the doorway, Rollison from the step which led down from the dining alcove to the living-room itself. Katherine was framed against the Trophy Wall, and the noose of the rope was just above her head.

Into this tense silence, the telephone rang with harsh, demanding loudness. Katherine started. Jolly raised his hands, then disappeared, going to answer at the extension. Rollison didn't move. The harsh ringing sound seemed to go on for a long time, then broke off. He could hear the sound of Jolly's voice, but not his words. They stopped, and there was a ting of the telephone bell as he replaced the receiver. His footsteps sounded.

"Can you spare me a moment, sir?" he asked from the doorway leading to the kitchen.

"Yes," said Rollison. Katherine's eyes were open but she did not seem to be looking as Rollison went to Jolly, and stepped inside the passage.

Jolly whispered, and the sibilants must have reached Katherine.

"Miss Oliver has come round, sir, and is out of danger. You might find that useful as a further means of persuasion."

"Yes, indeed," said Rollison, and his heart lifted. "There's one thing you've forgotten though; I might be wrong! Alec Dangerfield might be involved in all of this, and both women might be trying to make sure that no one ever proves it."

"I understand, sir," said Jolly. "I'll—*be careful, sir*."

Rollison spun round.

Katherine had backed to the Trophy Wall, and stood for a moment with a knife in her hand, a throwing knife once taken from a circus performer who had deliberately allowed his hand to slip. She was stepping towards the door, and so drawing nearer to Rollison. There was something both menacing and pathetic in her attitude, in this silent admission of guilt, in the forlorn attempt to frighten.

"I shouldn't, Kate," he said. "It isn't worth it."

"Don't come any nearer," Katherine warned. "Don't come any nearer."

"Give it up, give me the knife, and tell us the truth about Alec," urged Rollison, and went forward with his hand outstretched. He saw the way her face was distorted, and the glitter in her eyes, knew she was going to throw it, knew that she was on the edge of despair, knowing that she really had no choice, now.

She flung the knife.

It went inches wide, and after it clattered against the wall and fell, it caught the edge of the table, and dragged knives and forks and a glass with it; they fell tinkling. She ran towards the door, but Rollison was there ahead of her, holding her very closely as she writhed and kicked and tried to butt him with her head. He increased the pressure of his arms so that she was hugged tightly against him, her whole body paralysed. Quite suddenly she stopped straining to get free, and he let her go and asked again:

"Where is Alec?"

She said in a dead voice: "He's alive. He's in a room in a flat above his brother's flat in Mitten Court. He doesn't know that I'm involved, he thinks that his brother and Shawn are responsible. You are quite right. He discovered what was happening, and tried to stop it. I persuaded him to give his brother a chance. He promised not to tell the police, but Claude didn't trust him, and kept him prisoner. Then you began to worry Benoit."

She stopped; her whole body was motionless.

"If Alec's alive," said Rollison, "I shall leave it to the police to handle the case. I won't tell them that you told me where to find your husband."

She didn't answer.

"Is Percy Wrightson due tonight?" Rollison asked Jolly.

"Yes, sir, he should be here at any time."

"You and he look after Mrs. Dangerfield," said Rollison. "I'll go to Mitten Mews."

.　　　.　　　.　　　.　　　.

He found the upstairs in darkness. The police were no
longer in possession of the flat below, for nothing was left
there to incriminate Claude Dangerfield, and there had
been no reason to believe that he knew anything about the
small flat above his own. There was a modern lock, and
it took Rollison ten minutes to open it. He stepped inside,
and put on the light. There was a large living room here,
obviously used very little, for a film of dust lay every-
where. A door led to a kitchen, and he could see the sink.
Another door was closed. He went to this, and found it
locked. He used his pick lock, and it took only seconds to
open.

Inside, a bed was squeezed up in the corner of a room
which had only a tiny window, a room which smelt
stuffy and foul. He switched on the light, and saw the
man lying on the bed, bound to it, and with a cloth tight
round his mouth. The man's eyes were screwed up
against the strong light, and he cringed away, as if in fear,
believing that this was one of his captors.

Rollison began to cut the bonds.

When he had done this, and taken away the gag, he
realised that this was a skeleton of a man, whose cheeks
were hollow, whose mouth was deeply ridged by the cruelly
tight gag. Dangerfield looked more like a creature out of
Belsen than a human being, and he could make only a
few inarticulate sounds.

His bitch of a wife had done this to him.

Rollison almost wished she were here, so that he could
get his fingers round her throat.

He persuaded Alec Dangerfield that he was free from

fear, and went to a telephone in the big room and dialled Whitehall 1212. He reported what he had found, without mentioning Katherine Dangerfield, and waited in the street until police swung into the mews. He slipped away without being noticed, and went straight back to his flat. As he walked slowly up the stairs, he hardly knew what to think or what to hope.

The door opened as he reached it.

"Hallo, Jolly," Rollison said, and answered an unspoken question. "He was there, a living skeleton, but at least he is alive."

"I am very glad, sir," said Jolly, standing aside.

"I wonder if we should be. What happened here?"

"As you expected, I think," Jolly said quietly.

"Did she kill herself?"

"Yes, sir."

"How?"

"She had curare poison tablets in her bag, sir, and swallowed a tablet." Jolly led the way into the big room, and Rollison had a shock of surprise when he saw that it was empty. "She asked for the bathroom, and I felt it wise to take no precautions. I trust that I did the right thing."

"Yes," said Rollison slowly, "I'm sure you did. I only hope that Alec Dangerfield thinks so, too."

.   .   .   .   .

He saw Dangerfield at a nursing home, next day. The man was little more than skin and bone, but was still mentally alert and must have tremendous stamina—as his wife had. He had named his brother, called for his wife, and been told that she was ill. He recognised Rollison, and in a husky voice he thanked him, but he did not ask for details; for the time being all he wanted was rest.

.   .   .   .   .

Three months later, Alec was at the trial of his brother, of the man who had helped his brother at Rollison's flat, and of Morrison. By that time, he knew everything about his wife, what she had done, how she had died. He also knew that he owed his life to her; she had kept him alive, for with him alive she had one trump to use if Claude turned on her, as she knew he would all the others. Alec looked an entirely different person physically, lean but not thin, hardy and tanned from several weeks convalescence in France, alert, and if not particularly handsome, striking to look at. He was called to give evidence against his brother and Morrison, explained that he had found the stores of forged money in the vaults, after following Morrison to them one night. He had challenged Morrison about it, and then been kidnapped. He was in court when his brother and the other man were sentenced to death and Morrison to life imprisonment.

Rollison saw him leave the Old Bailey with Betty Oliver, who had lost a lot of weight.

Rollison went straight to Gresham Terrace, with Jolly, and the door was opened by Percy Wrightson, who was bursting with news.

"That Dangerfield bloke rung up, Mr. Ar, said he was coming rahnd at half past four. That's in an hour's time. I said as far as I knew you was coming straight home."

"Fine," said Rollison.

"Slap up tea, that's what they'll need today," Wrightson declared. "Everything seems better on a full stomach, that's what I always say. Shall I nip out for some cream?"

Alec Dangerfield arrived just before half past four with Betty Oliver. It was good to see that Betty was quite calm and composed, and the loss of weight suited her.

"We're not going to stay long, Mr. Rollison," Dangerfield said, "but I felt that Betty and I couldn't leave the country without seeing you. I've sold the agency, as you may know, and I'm putting all the proceeds as well as much of my personal fortune against losses which shareholders and customers made in the New World Travel Association. I feel that's the least I can do. Betty and I will get married quietly, when we reach New York. I am joining a small firm in New York. I think it's much better if I get off to a fresh start."

"I'm sure you couldn't be more right," Rollison said, and smiled at Betty Oliver. "May I ask just one question?"

"Ask as many as you like, I'm quite immune now," Betty said. "I promise that I won't try to scratch your cheeks, either."

"Thanks! Why did you say that Alec had told you to take those files?"

"Kate told me he was hidden away, and said that if I didn't get them he would just be left there to die," answered Betty. "It—it was the only chance I had to help him, so I had to take it."

"Yes, of course," said Rollison, and smiled faintly, and asked: "When Kate gave you the morphine tablets in your coffee, why didn't you refuse to drink it? You realised she had poisoned you, didn't you?"

After a pause, Betty answered huskily: "Yes, I did, but —it was a case of dying or of telling Alec the truth if he ever got free. Kate told me that he didn't know she was involved, that he only knew about his brother. She told me that if we got those files it would be impossible for the police to question anyone who knew she had been involved, and that provided Alec could never find out, she would release him. I didn't know whether to believe her, I could only pray that she was telling the truth. And I thought it was better for Alec that he should never know, that the police should never question me. You see," she added very quietly, "I knew that I wouldn't be able to stand up to questioning."

"You thought Alec's best chance of survival would be for you to die," said Rollison. "Is that it?"

Betty didn't answer; Dangerfield's eyes were radiant.

Rollison said: "I hope you'll be the happiest couple in the world."

They had left, happy as they could be, when the telephone bell rang, and Rollison answered the call. A man with a broad Yorkshire voice said:

"Ah bet your doan't remember me, Mr. Rollison," and in a flash Rollison's mind went back to the Rue de Rivoli, and to the Yorkshireman whose French had been so good and timely.

"I'd forgotten you, but I won't again," Rollison said warmly. "Will you and your wife come and have dinner with me tonight?"

"We'll be right happy to," the Yorkshireman said. "I'm hoping you'll tell us all about it, Mr. Toff."

He and his wife listened, enthralled . . .

And as it happened, it was on the following morning that an air mail post card from Sydney reached the Toff. It read, briefly:

"*Do hope you got the money back. Please let me know. Mike and I love it here.*"

Rollison read this twice, smiled, took a drawing pin from his desk, and pinned the card to the Trophy Wall.

THE END